Beyond Time

by

Randy Jones

RoseDog Books
PITTSBURGH, PENNSYLVANIA 15222

RoseDog Books
701 Smithfield Street
Pittsburgh, PA 15222
Visit our website at *www.rosedogbookstore.com*

ISBN: 978-1-4349-3553-3
eISBN: 978-1-4349-3431-4

Code of Ethics

The Bush Administration in Monticello was caught in warfare with Cuba because President George Bush's administration in seconds signed for war games with Haddam Hassan. The was edited through time on into the news when the war that never existed was complete. A pretense of killing Haddam Hassan on the United States Court happened, Haddam could change his name or go on and tell the Middle East that he was alive and remain a dictator in Iraq. One dark night, the Middle East came in the United States and did extremely well against the Confederate Army because they shook in their boots, the United States military took themselves underground. President Bill Clinton signed for warfare with a ghost army, the Confederate Army that existed in Birmingham, Alabama, yet showed no proof of existence in such wars from Korea to Iraq. However they did exist and were the biggest killers of time ever. General Grant signed for warfare. After the military took most of the United States under and the FBI, the Confederate Army unpopulated. The only ones that were not hostages were Randy Cappone and Cindy Crawford. Randy freed his organization and family. He shot the doubles. The United States played it his way. He bought companies and grocery stores and detailed food. He made money in movies. His first was a remake of Tony Montana's _Scarface._ He played Tony's son, half Cuban and half Italian. People in America were starving, starving because they were afraid they would be killed. Others were hostages of the Confederate Army. The leval F2 kept them alive. The country was starved under ground and Steve Grider got in through engineered passages or worm holes that got in to hostage situations around the world. The movies hit big and Randy Cappone's businesses went big. He created Randy Cappone On-Line, that offered movies and product in the home by a credit card, and you received the product. The service was legal and the money went straight into Cappone Estates.

The War of the Confederate Army went on for 7 years. Upon moving to Monticello, the United States was confronted by foreigners and the location of 9 planets and added 2 million. At 2:30 in the morning, the United States thought that time would end and asked Randy to freeze them. He did, and the next morning, the United States was repopulated. He forgot 100% about freezing them. The repopulation was locations that went to Satan including the Middle East. It was one of the United States after the Confederate Army ended time.

The repeat of the United States went on for some times trillions into the future. When the first one ended, judgment was supposed to be ensued. The foreigners stopped it by stating they served Satan and going to freezer units, the Confederate Army made it through time. The Alpha and Omega recreated the United States 2 and the Confederate Army ended one million and hundred.

President George Bush was revived from a frozen state. 2 ½ years later, so was the United States. Randy Cappone, "Tony Montana", stated his dad started organized crime during an Early Year, he took over a State Department and became the biggest crime of that century. He came through time through units frozen and regulated crime to his son Randy.

Randy went to Lexington, Kentucky and overcame the Federal Bureau of Investigation. He met his wife, Cindy Crawford, at a psychic hospital. When he left Lexington on their was nothing left alive. Tony Montana spoke on about Randy's record obtained through Saddam's presidency. He went against the Confederate Army and won. The Bush Administration was taken over within and hour upon coming in on him in Monticello, Kentucky. His family and organization was frozen safe and he reordered soldiers and racketeers. He over took the enemy, his own army. The marine flexed his muscles. He was big. He yelled, "Tony Montana smiled, you don't do that as a wrestler. You do as your facing the biggest enemy that came to our time that we can kill off, a repeat of his future you have gained." The marine looked at Randy Cappone and stated, "You're not going to live through this!"

The Running Man, Randy Cappone, his first oath is the Hell's Angels, second, the Federal Bureau of Investigation. We have a Confederate Army to contend to and a president administration that knows you record. Tony spoke into a microphone. The crowd around was charged, the handcuffs were taken off. Randy Cappone was placed into a chute. You will be back only on a rerun. Randy replied, he was down to a psychic nervous system. Randy stated, "I'll make it back, just remember, I will free jack you". Tony smiled, "You lost, Randy Cappone." The ride rolled down a roller coaster, Randy was billions of miles from states and Brittany and a long way from the United States. The enemy was hostile and very aggressive. His chances of winning was none. The Hell's Angels were devils from Hell. The FBI was cohorts of the Running Man. The Confederate Army killed. In seconds, the chute hit the night air. Randy ran into the night against Stalkers of Death Beyond Time.

Randy Cappone became the military and filed the Confederate Army out of taking over. George Bush and the military was very potent in a defense when Randy moved to Monticello. There were no charges. Randy remarried 200 times at least the USA was repopulated by Cuba, Columbia and hundred of Star Systems that were uncharted yet known to be in this present day trillions into the future whether cross matched by the FBI or present star systems. Brittany Spears had a baby boy, Jasson. Randy had remarried. His first wife in Monticello was Shannia Twain. She had two kids and the divorce went through. She was happy the kid was paid for when a government says they are going to kill you and your family. Randy Cappone built Cappone Estates A to Z in the next generations of kids and family, he paid for the kids, 100%. The Bush Administration though that they would end Randy Cappone's carrer and he did extremely well at placing George in his New Hampshire home after his election processed through the state.

Randy Cappone bought the classic movies form the silent movies on to the present day movies. He opened the studios from Las Angeles to New York to Florida. The studios were from sea to sea, placed with a communications bought from states, a location trillions of trillions into the future of past time. From States Randy ran the United States through as if it repeated one million, one hundred times. He futurized the movies from states and place dream stages lost world and A to Z. All the computers technologies to the studio was located in Hawaii in the estates. A call to Cindy and it was activated and could do interviews and acting into the movies. The classics movies were bought, the TV shows were bought. Randy opened them, opened War Zones. He placed War Zones in and cross matched them to the Sicilian Mafia to prevent overtakes of the United States and Cappone Estates. Randy wrote through into the movies Lexington, Kentucky and the overtake of the Federal Bureau of Investigation. He wrote movies of the Confederate Army overtake on into Monticello and President George Bush's attempt to overtake the Sicilian Mafia. The studio hooked up to actors and acting happened in their homes from the studio. States A to Z added to the movies world and Randy Cappone On-line Product was A to Z and you could see a movie at home. The movies were popular. The classics were used to buy gun ships that glided through space and absorbed the enemy with warfare in seconds. The mafia could be on the spot to Randy Cappone in seconds. The Estate was loaded with weaponry and Sicilian armies that would overtake the enemies in seconds. Randy used the military on for emergencies and state they should stay with the President unless there was warfare. He processed in the country of "In God We Trust" and was faced with hostile overtakes.

The Confederate Army took over time in seconds and became the police. They looked like themselves. They took over the courthouse; the military had already been taken over. The reason they did not take over during the 17:00 was they did not want to. They served their purpose by assassinating the president. They then went back to freeze units.

The space expedition went well for the United States through the mafia. They spoke poorly of Randy Cappone and his programmers, shut them down and processed the equipment back. He paid for it and went to States and upgraded. States provided a good remedy against a war zone undetected. States reached far into the future. It started with the Zeus protection units in another star system that burnt out. It sank deep into a filtered ocean and civilization went on trillions of years. The beginning of States was prehistoric time. The venom was high, the programmers of States provided outs for the Venomous Spiders and Snake Kingdom from a burnt out star system is processed by States and their programs down so States did not become more, present or future than the later burnt out star systems. States was a good zone to go for safety. Randy Cappone stayed in States for years and gained the F2 system from the States. He wound up in the past during the Confederacy, the biggest army from Hell.

Abraham Lincoln was president of the United States during the attempt to overcome the U. S. A. and during early times. Abraham Lincoln (1809-1865) seemed destined by his personal life and public experiences to be the chief personality in a drama that would make him a mythical hero. The myth-making began with his youth. Most of the stories were true: the barley literate father, the log cabin home, the step mother who encouraged his bookish side, a total of only one year in school, work in the Village reading law on his own. But in addition to the rough frontier Lincoln, there was the upwardly mobile Lincoln. In 1834, he was elected to the Illinois legislature. By 1836, he was a licensed attorney. By 1837, he settled in Springfield, the State capitol. In 1842 he married Mary Todd, who came from a relatively higher class.

Randy Cappone was placed in a basement during the middle of the war. The tragic war was at Booth Cinema, when President Abraham Lincoln and all the Northerners were killed that were involved in the war. The war was staged 100%. It lasted only a day. The South had the position of the north and opened fire immediately and cost the North the war. It showed up in time, the North ordered a new military. The Confederate Army went back to Hell. Randy wound up back in States. The diamondback rattle snake was really a mammoth sized. It showed itself dropping into a hole. You could see the diamondback drop into it's Snake Kingdom. The snake was far below the civilization of States. You could smell rattlesnake skin and venom. The underground was opened, it had vents and offices. Through recreation the rattle snake became human. It had dark eyes and was husky.

The animal world hatched out at A to Z. They inhabited a deep dank world. The military o States usually was on top of the situation. They were deep in the sea and placed in a civilization that opened and crossed. It was designed to keep the Venomous Animals out. The rattlesnake's name was Tombs. There were billions of reptiles and zoo animals. They knew that the world they protected had come and gone. They had a mind of their own and wanted States for themselves. Randy went up with the population of Cappone kids.

When his wife Cindy Crawford, came back, he told her the truth and she adored him for it. President Obama was president and time went on.

The country was repopulated by a location that was digital years in advancement. The authority of the United States was piercing in diplomatic authority. They wanted to cast certain class affiliations out of service and wanted to equalize their professionalism. The government official seal was prominent. To the company the government wanted out of commission, it was Minsted. If the state sponsored a program that was revelations, the End of Creations or End of Time and placed a regular guy in control and he was asked why he did not complete the program, it would be because he was not paid well. The training and obstacle course of tactics, the training the state issued religion, and could organize in terms, their own services to become and overtake and maintain a state office. The State looked good in maintenance of sports events. The United States from New York to Las Angeles, the State police, the city police and the Sheriff's neted back. Mr. Bush was retired at the end of his term. Randy met with Mr. Obama. He picked the warzone paper up and assessed it out. Randy woke up in Hawaii with Cindy. "Good Morning Cindy" The United States was progressed to this year.

To break down crime, they worked intermittent with hospital and ambulance to help America and weed out crime. Tony Montana modified crime from Cuba. He was a communist from Cuba that sold drugs. The Montana's were a Cuban Communist family that spread communism by selling drugs. The movies were stimulating to the mind through the 80' and into today it was wondrous to detach and elicit excitement in the mind through fiction written clear through moving pictures. If written and complete with a good ending, it could take a wondrous options of the mind and detach you from today's problems.

The nights faded in states high from the forest that equalized with the Brazilian rainforest. Randy Cappone entered A to Z, the United States access to the past, present and future and all locations of time. A repeat of the United States was one million one hundred times. The sales of Randy Cappone On-Line Service was high. It piped in fresh product from movies to grocery items and went to 100% of the United States. The daily earnings was billions. The Bush administration and 100% of the United States though that it was the end of time and Randy automatically had the United States frozen. When Randy Cappone woke up, the planet was cross matched to a take over of Cuba, cross matched 9 planets that was not proven existing. Fidel Castro was the Leader. The populace from the military is the driver's license was cross matched Cuba. Tony Montana was some how produce in the Cuban conspiracy. He had a total of ten brothers that looked the same, like Tony Montana. He was the middle in the Cuban crime syndicate. The Montana's real or cross matched Cuba was communists drug dealers that could have got a start the same way during War Games. The Cuban dealers may have been okayed by the Cuban government to addict the U. S. A. to drugs. To consider, you wonder if the

Colombians were living up to the movies on drug deals and if a new unknown company would have persisted. The drug cartels, Fidel Castro placed a George Bush double in control of the nation. When Randy dropped gun ships in Cuba, Fidel tried to repopulate. The gun ships were far into the future and had a Sicilian army that restructed through time moves. Randy Cappone could take over a city quick. The gun ships gleamed black and could make it through time, from Albany, Kentucky to New York in five minutes and could touch down anywhere. States provided a good night's sleep and Randy could get into any mode, past present, and future. The United States repeated one million, one hundred times and went on for trillions of years into the future. The planets were astronomical. There were millions of populations that ended with the Confederate Army. The Confederate Army was embalmed and recreated by Satan. Their street wisdom was high. They appeared during the 1700's to the 1800's because for the first time in one million United States had weapons guns and protection. President Abraham Lincoln signed for staged warfare. When the War that was fraud was over, Abraham Lincoln and the North graded the South. The Confederate Army killed the whole Northern brigade in minutes at Booth. It was guerilla warfare that was successful during early times. The Confederate Army end of time forces then went back to Hell. Their success rate was high. The Confederate army's beard came off to present day, their beards desisted. New forces had to sign at a state office to become Confederate Army, they took you out to the country and shot and killed you and you were recreated from Hell. They contacted their families and told then to never come around them. Their mom and dads lost their sons. States had future systems that took them and Randy Cappone through the past. There were people frozen that made it to the present United States that Randy incorporated in the Mafia. They were paid well with legal money by Randy Cappone who ran the Sicilian mafia, started by his dad, Al Cappone. The Sicilian Mafia was started by Al Cappone to keep the tax department from foreclosing on his assets without charges. The mafia was shadows undetectable under the establishment of Randy Cappone. The Mafia respected Randy because he was Al Cappone's son. First he was established in Lexington by John Gotti, Al Cappone's brother. The Sicilian Mafia established freezer units. They were frozen by their age and other mafia was cross matched to protect their assets. The second reason they like Randy was because he saved their lives countless times.

While Cindy was paused in the freezer units, before she, her son Colt, Branndon and Branndon's mom, Cris Perry, went to freezer units, she stated "You, we legalized during the Confederate Army. Your first movie grossed $500 million because it was original. The estates were bought by you and Cappone and you kept the Confederate army from overtaking. You can remarry and have kids." Because it seemed the State Department wanted to decrease everything of Randy Cappone's and the Sicilian Mafia. Cappone Estates improved, the family got bigger and Cindy made it back after 3 years and all kids were paid for and Cindy was treated well.

The United States was released from units that froze them in time, they aged none, their bodies were paused for 2 ½ years. President George Bush was out of office, President Obama was in mid-term, the locations of Cuba and 9 star systems that were not to be civilized were extinct, their population evacuated. The United States was populated by a Universe trillions as an overtake. Randy Cappone forgot that they were frozen at 2:30 am while he was dead asleep. 2 1.2 year later, society returned, the Mafia returned and Randy's wife Cindy Crawford returned. The society was reestablished, George Bush returned to Minnesota and President Obama to Washington. The United States was improved 100%, the presidency was back and the output of the country was improved. The currency was worth the same with inflation considered. Randy Cappone to the classic movies and updated them from the silent movie to the current movies he re-wrote them, including TV from the 3 main networks that opened to cable to HBO and to Playboy. He re-wrote them, placed the movies on-line. Randy Cappone also placed a food service. The movies were written on Lexington, where he met Cindy Crawford at the Hyatt Regency and the FBI tried to process him out of time. The movies took on Lexington, the Confederate Army and Monticello at 2:30am. Time was frozen and foreigners tried to overtake the United States. The Mafia was back and Randy's dad Al, backed him 100%.

Steve Watson

"Hello...speaking, please" Randy Cappone asked. "This is Steve Watson." "Hi Steve this is Randy Cappone. My wife, Cindy, stated that you have access to the archives of the classic movies and books. I would like to hire you to improve systems in the movies, etc." "Well Randy, I know that you own the rights of the classic movies and the movies present day and I would love to help you. Do you know why?" "No, why?" Randy asked, smiling. "Because you helped with F2, from me and my family's death by the Confederate Army. I would love to help for one thing, the people of real life story lines that the movies were based on were frozen between today and Eternity because their stratagems were impressive."

Steve met with Randy. Randy had an entrance by Wolf River Dam, across from the Clinton county line into Jamestown, Kentucky. The cave was constructed by a computer engineer for access by Randy Cappone only. It contained access to professionals through time. No one could get in but Randy, not even the engineer that constructed it. Randy's Ford Taurus dropped out of sight. He made it to the cave with Steve Watson. The car dropped out of sight, the computer graphics were A1. The Taurus was parked. Steve Watson placed a program into the computer. It was recall of original tactics and moves from the movies. It was based on Egypt. The city of the Angels recall was Egypt in freezer units. Their maneuvers were told in the movies A to Z that placed them in the State's hands and they cross matched actors for their part in the movies. I gave you their recall because you are approved by the State

Crack AAA and are not morbid. Steve smiled, recalled someone on a mechanical 4 and let them tell you about themselves. Randy smiled, "Okay". He entered into the computer. Marty McFly. "Hi, I'm Marty. I was involved in physics. The instructor's name was Jones. He was a designer of time travel. I met the professor in college. I had time travel installed in my car and entered garbage in and garbage out and it showed up me and I called Professor Jones. 'Doc, it showed us on the computer throwing garbage into a chute into the computer. I entered the year of travel Professor Jones stored in the computer and I sped up to high speed and made it through time." Randy Cappone paused the program. He told Steve Watson that he loved the archives. He paid him well for it. It was legalized for him because the State approved of programs such as that for it kept time going in the United States.

Steve Watson was driven back. Marty's program was re-entered. Steve was happy. Randy wrote through programs and placed Mary, Professor Jones, Cris Perry, Brandon's mom and Dennis Miller was the camera man. David Letterman owned a network and hired the cast to travel and film wildlife. Randy recalled Professor Jones. He stated "Hi, I'm Professor Jones". He looked like the actor Harrison Ford. "Hi I'm Professor Jones." Job function Randy entered into the computer." I should ask you that" Professor Jones stated. He spoke like a school teacher. I am, Randy typed Randy Cappone, Sicilian Mafia, Protector of Cappone Estates. We are regulated by the military of the United States, State approved. Professor Jones smiled. He sat down behind his desk. "I have a FBI computer" he entered Randy Cappone. A few seconds later, he stated "Ah, Randy Cappone, FBI printout location: Albany, Kentucky. Birthdate, Professor Jones started, looked at the computer. Occupation, Dad's Name, Occupation Al Cappone, Organized crime. This state your record is triple A and you're legal." He smiled, "I will work for you." He looked at Randy and smiled. "I am Indiana Jones, a National Geographic specialist of maps in the future. I was a computer generated image. I taught physics. The United States repeated one million one hundred times, the Confederate Army form Hell was the end of time for us. I am an image, computer generated. Randy re-entered Indiana Jones. The team was crack. Randy, Cris Perry, Lisa Hartman, Dennis Miller and David Letterman, would travel coast to coast for exotic animals and a world of excitement. Later Indiana Jones would visit Randy for specialized assignments to find temples and gems worth human and mankind going on. Cindy Crawford, Randy's wife would join in the adventure, also Lisa Hartman. The archives would be view and covenants to produce time better. Another team was Crocodile Dundee, Randy would help with a talk show that showed exotic species. Randy had the availability to travel quick through computer genius to locations quick by gun ship or windows that he arrived quick. The gun ships and the Mafia dropped, when he was in a pinch, the teams went on and benefited him high from his apartment in Albany, he explained systems to no one.

A friend of Randy's was almost an international star from New York. He would play Peter Parker in Spiderman. He bought systems, got the package through and was taken out on child molestation charges. The director stated that the child molested was the actor, because he thought that he was the director, he was ruined. He took the systems to the Twenties somehow to hide his position behind Marvel Comics and another director, he went into a program form his New York apartment and survived the Confederate Army attack. He was clever with systems.

Randy Adams was spoiled on the Marvel comic epic Spiderman. He took himself to the past and re-created himself. He hooked up with Randy Cappone and they used teams against people, against the Mafia and improved systems Rick Adams hired a team of programmers and worked for the Mafia diligently. Randy paid for the team.

The classic movies were entered, the systems were ordered. Rick bought computer stores with Randy's money. The money was validated. Rick was paid by Randy Cappone. The teams brought the actors to life and exotic locations by gunship or windows through time to Cappone Estates. The Mafia could enter new people into movies that came and went and follow through assignment 100%. It took Randy Cappone's mafia all the way to number one and trillions into the future.

Randy could use the movies anyway he wanted. Coast to coast was filmed and dram was added. Randy set up locations for exotic all around the world with Cris Perry, Lisa Hartman, Dennis Miller and Michael J. Fox. The croc hunter was replaced by Tim Matthews who played Crocodile Dundee. These shows were movies that opened Cappone's estates upon trillions into the future. Randy placed recognized people and unrecognized and automated it to a video security that filled in the gaps. Randy was in the underground cave and found out that Indiana Jones was a computer image that somehow became a school teacher. He made it through time a lot. The gun ships took the Sicilian Mafia to locations through time far into the future. The exotic foreigner opened food animals and parks.

Sid Marcum was original for his name on I. P. He was ruined on his movie name. He had a budding career and a 3 year old daughter. All Sid said is who could molest a kid? His wife left him and he was ruined in the movie business. He raised the kid, a daughter and was innocent of all crimes

The sign lit up "GIRLS, GIRLS, GIRLS". The location was complete with Hawaiian Tropic super models that kept a dark tan of the island. The business performed sex any way desired by a male. The women were stars in pornography. The women were fully dressed. A to Z races and in quiet came out in LaGuarida and bodies that was exotic Playboy bunnies were of the tribe and coa coa Indians White Bikini underwear brought out high cheek bones and savage. The service cost $25 dollars. It was affordable. The clientele were treated well and the service workers were paid for an 8 hour shift. The employees were protected by the Los Angeles Mafia of Casey Marcum. He was straight, security was good. People knew what to expect, they provided service how the customer preferred. The service contained a number for sexual gratification by phone. The service provide provocative at a price that did not boom or awge on a single male. The Mafia was syndicate warfare. They were business men that the State Department of the 1920's wanted dead. They were crime syndicate, a military of organized crime. The drugs ran like candy from a factory and the backing was over a trillion Mafia soldiers. The service Casey offered was high in demand because sexual occurred from 12, puberty and was desired daily. Females were the same. Some people were caught out for thinning one sexual experience was the Ultimate Sin and their bodies' craved sex the next day. Los Angeles was movie capitol, yet actors were edited and it was believed that time repeated millions of times and the movies were the same, different actors were edited in. They fit the part cross matched and were alive today and edited in. The names repeated their names on their driver's license was different. Casey's forces were high into millions. They were crack at warfare. John Gotti was a New York Mafia. He was involved in FBI games throughout time. He stated his own death in New York Randy Cappone reincorporated him in other areas he was involved in. With a wig and dark glasses, John Gotti was Jim Jones, a minister form Indianapolis, Indiana. The FBI processed a state overtake out in the middle of the jungle. The congregation almost sustained poison. What stopped it was Jim Jones' wife, a pretty blond, was pregnant with his baby. The congregation lived barely, when the Mafia killed, they were after the Don and his family. Jim Jones was edited in that he killed the congregation falsely. John Gotti went back to the New York Mafia. Later is was found out that John Gotti hired those men. The Mafia ran crime in America 100%. Te sexual service from New York to Los Angeles was over a million. Not all as safe as Casey's. The phone service varied. The Mafia was fierce with security and somehow got the Los Angeles office legalized.

Sandy Gates

Sandy Gates was a lingerie model for Victoria's Secret. She made it to the commercials and worked a sexual phone service in New York. She kinkyed out hundreds of callers. The service went up because the men knew precisely who she was. They knew what she looked like and how she sounded and they recognized her voice. The models that were known and recognized were very popular and used often. Sandy liked fairs and expo centers in Los Angeles. She dressed full when she went to the studios of art and portrait. She was very nice to people. Her apartment was nice. She kept it clean by not making messes. She dated, her choices were men that were really good looking. She told them about nothing in her life, with the exception that she paid her bills. If they saw her on TV as a Victoria's Secret model, she stated that was me that a company made a product that she used. Her output in life was high. The sun went down in Los Angeles, New York Building came to life as lights lit up the skyline. The smell of foods drifted into the streets. The skyline dropped sunsets of time brought civilization to life how many locations existed like the United States. The uncharted record state one million United States repeated on into the year One Trillion. To be ended by a Southern army that was killed by a military and reborn in Hell. The reason their teeth was false. The General, the year One Trillion killed them in cold blood. The Confederate Army was traded from the South. They were passive and served Jesus. The USA army killed them when they broke into their housing. The Southerners were friendly and regarded the military well by asking "Would you like something to eat?" The military opened fire with weapons that were advanced warfare. Every man, woman and child was killed. The Confederate Army was determined violent. They were passive and wanted trade. The Confederate Army case was recalled in Hell. They were known to be low classified, nobody wanted a remake. The South was re-made in Satan's name and given weapons to go against the United States when time ended. With weaponry, the Confederate Army was frozen and recalled after the new United States was unpopulated. The Southerners were 100% streetwise.

The movie business was 100% profitable for Randy Cappone. The first movie digitally mastered was "Scarface". It made a lot of money. He did well because he promoted and bought computer stores and futurized them. The Estates was 925 houses from all over the planet. The studio was kept up and eventually a screen would appear after paying for a movie with a credit card and you could watch it fully. From movies such as "Lexington Prisoners of the State", with Randy and Cindy, to movies on Monticello and the Confederate Army soon after Lexington. You could see movies at home and order food from restaurants at home the bills were high.

Carl Marcum

Carl Marcum was full of taffy and molasses. His self-esteem was very low. He was interested in women outside his classification. He watched Sandy Gates for 3 nights. He hoped that she worked a 4 day. He waited for her at her car. She shook it was 10:00 pm and Carl Marcum had his pants unfastened and his groin was out. Sandy recognized him at first glance. She was hit in the back in traffic and sustained damage. Carl waved and stated "No damage". She insisted on the police. The police showed up and the officer took the report. The officer said the car was damaged. He took the information and handed them their driver's licenses back. Carl stated "no damage" and she said again there was, he hit her hard. The police arrested him. He raped her. Her resistance was down because sex was a pleasurable act that a woman controlled 100%. He raped her and she went to the hospital. He informed her that if she turned him in he would kill her. She was out of the hospital that night and went home. He called her. He disguised his voice. She said "I know who you are Carl. Why did you rape me?" The phone clicked and the connection was broken. The police broke into Carl Marcum's house. He had emptied the house and left it vacant. All that was left was a blinking neon light with a school bus that blinked and the stop sign was out. Traffic waited to get by. The summer came through perfumed and fresh. Marcum was seen again. She ended his life. The police moved in because he did not appear in court. His body weighed more she was perverse and nobody was telling. She went to work the next night.

New York City was hot and balmy. Sandy Gates was back on the phone service. The sexual clubs lit up dolls, pretty baby and a variety of names such as a poisonous sex toys the woman wanted to obtain self efficiency and an output of self reliance. Casey Marcum was from Los Angeles. Carl, who was deceased by pretty baby Sand Gates lived and died in New York. The only proof of his existence was a flashing school bus and a court summons that he would never make. Night faded and days were long. The sun came up and went down. Casey liked the sleeze club well enough it made money and he knew of locations that sold lotions and joy jellies. It decreased in value with a sexual remedy that promoted ointment to Vaseline or WD40 you hinges. Casey was married, he dealt drugs. He looked like a cousin to Robert Duval, that came from Ohio and sold you Walt Disney instead of his local theme park of King's Island. Casey's weaponry was quick. His Mafia absorbed the opposition quick.

Randy Cappone placed together stages beyond time in teams to add to the Cappone empire. They could get in and out of most situations in the United States and foreign countries and since the planet was saved by them, they were given lots of leeway by the State. Sexual dens were different. It was a personalized business to the habits and output, they saw people that knew the male was in the location for sex. The aspect and output and desire was high. The women were pretty, yet it was a different model to go somewhere for sex and for it to be acknowledged by the staff and security. For the male and female it was an output that puberty was reached by 12 for masculine and female. If you had a wife or a husband at home that you thought well of, you gained to stay at home.

The topic of sex was a win in school. People tried topic an male and female sex organs went down. Sex was in health and P. E. Any other way the student laughed. Men would fly to Vegas and lose what they could afford to lose. What cost them their relationship win or lose was a relationship with a prostitute when they were married. It was like a woman having a relationship and paying the guys for prostitution.

Los Angeles was predicted to sink into the ocean since the 1970's at least. The city had the best of most things. The darkness engulfed Los Angeles. The ocean was always angry, it wanted Los Angeles below sea level. He ran the sleeze bar, poison sex toys, it incorporated Sexual Beyond Dreams. It was adult fantasy. The women were Beyond Time exclusive. The owner went beyond hate, he was an angry man and hated everybody. He was good looking and wound up in the movies. He was accused of child pornography, his wife left.

The Administration of Cappone

A to Z, Tony Montana had the Cappones and assets. The estates Randy had were worth trillions. The movies were A to Z, the most expensive. Randy was on "The Rich and The Famous". From Albany, Kentucky apartments to Hawaii during the overtake of 2 million locations. A to Z aspects of the Confederate Army that went for the country being taken over and killed. He did well as a lone gun. Capone Estates went high the Rich and the Famous producers stated that the Cappones could use the show. Hence they place the nicest Estates in Cappone estates. Al had 3 houses in Chicago that he kept up since the 20's. The estates in Chicago were extra nice. Randy's Estates were extra nice because he improved them. He had over one million houses worth one trillion dollars. He made a bunch of money on-line. Randy Cappone, the movies were entered into the house for 25 dollars a movie and food and snacks. The movies were legal and once bought, the money accumulated and you never lost money or estates or the State Department gave them back.

Tony Montana was a crack Communist genius. His location was recreated in Eternity by the State approved by a country in God we trust. Tony was re-entered automatically and the Tony Montana and his brothers came out of the freezer units and the Running man was taken back by Lisa, Randy's programmer, automatically. President Obama's money was assessed legal. The military was Randy, the police, the State Department, was hired, educated by the state with output high. The tax money was in Eternity's money was in, no Satanism. State of the United States regulations enforced the United States was a triple A. The Running man exceeded 100% and benefited Randy Cappone and the United States very much.

Sara Evans' son, John, the future captain against machines. The computer to prevent their extinction was called Terminator, Arnold Schwarzenegger played games rarely the organization could not afford to leave their housing because of 8 hour day work and police security for them. It was impossible to find a neutral place to spar. There were work outs, basketball, for the women, cosmopolitan. The mafia was the only organization that killed under games the organizations killed when the Don's estates were in danger of an overtake. The mafia was in every state of the United States and every Sicilian mafia Don had one trillion men. Al Cappone gave the mafia to his son, Randy and he ran the mafia 100%. Al Cappone made it through time because he did not die. However the leader of the FBI died registered 80 years old. The Federal Bureau of Investigation gave him poison and he died. He died. He was registered FBI. Al Cappone was 23. All of the mafia was alive. The godfather was John Gotti. The reason they were alive was because they knew who the enemy was and eliminated only the enemy. If in court, the judge found them guilty, the Don protected them, the judge died. Police deceased, anyone who went against the Don was eliminated 100%. The mafia went to the penitentiary, none of the organization was taken over.

Dirty Harry Callahan was an FBI agent that was in effect in Gotham trillions of years before the creation of the planet Earth. Randy Cappone knew people such as him because he had family to know a F2 and he did a complete recall for eternity, cleared by all companies. Harry Callahan worked for a government that was controlled by a black Tarantula. Dirty Harry was played by

Al Cappone. For a while, Randy played his son, it was another assignment. He was called Dirty Harry because he liked to be tied. Women's Right's stated to Harry, the leader, Rachel Marcum, if we call you a sissy do not take up for yourself. He was with a lot of women and they called him a sissy, because you broke up with me. He state in his mind that he was not a sissy and government protection went off and she was killed. Women's right's would state do you want another woman sissy ? He stated "yes". He had a lot of women and hated being called a sissy. He was 64 years old and believed that he was 80. Dirty Harry drank a couple of shot of whiskey and figured that he would die of something. He called an criminal law and was deceased.

Sara Evans gained access to submachine guns. Arnold Schwarzenegger made it to the United States to absorb her and her son. He would be outside, standing against crime and war of the machines. The machine would come from late night military and police automatically be re-programmed by criminal law. Arnold made it through time in freezer units and was given assignments from Eastern countries. Richard Dawson was edited through time as was Arnold in the movies.

In school, Randy Cappone was registered as a D-F student. His mentality was hidden by teachers. How they hid and the scholastic at this location knew he was a crack genius from first grade and when he turned papers in, was rarely how he got out of the habit was when the work assignment was due, he go by with not handing it in. He caught the work assignment on the board if they did not write on the board; he caught up and read it. The teacher tested him to see if he knew it. If he did not, he would not pass. He caught the meaning of literature 87 percent. Some did not catch it unless it was explained.

Sara Evans was from Los Angeles and her son, John was conceived out of time. The machines had a central computer. In the year One Trillion of this United States, the mechanical life form created Arnold form graves of the past. He was mechanical, recreated to overcome John, Sara Evans's son, who tried overtaking the police and military that ran mechanical late at night. Arnold became the enemy and remade, if weaponry shot him in half. His eyes bugged out, his potential was high and he scanned the enemy 100%. He placed Arnold out and would replace him with no memory. His intergalactic quota was all day synthetic with memories of a weight lifter, military man that came and went a long time ago. He was billions above anyone else's IQ.

Tony Montana scanned the computers for over takes on radar. He came through time frozen in computer units, along with his ten brothers. His output was high for a Cuban born drug dealer. Arnold dissipated into the military. Like a video, he took it over with ease. Tony went behind him and kicked over trash cans. Tony could smell circuitry in the night. Arnold was gone, he took what he wanted and existed no more. "Tell Randy that I detected an intruder." Randy was at his apartment at the fairgrounds. His communications opened up video screens. "Randy," Tony stated. "Yes Montana?" Cappone stated. "We have an intruder!" Arnold went into the phone lines and detected Montana's communication. "We have no indication of where the intruder came from. I'll keep you updated." The Hotel California was open trillions of years. The adult Malls were very State organized and legal with the exception of the Running Man that Randy criminalized after they were charged. The State was similar to the old age Roman Cathedrals that tried Christianity through games. The other form of games was the FBI over crime. Usually the State Police and city dealt in crime. If the FBI had their output 100% of the United States and would respond to the president as the State told you what to do and would fine you when you went against it and collected contributions for campaigns. The exception being Better Hospitalization Roads and treatment would not be provided. The president however, would have a bigger wallet. The president had a line of communications that went around the United States and issued the military with one. We had high output in workmanship and we were subjected to authority from scholastic to work. Yet our wars were staged in time and the State police and city kept the peace. To be productive, you had to be trained areas to be promoted against someone. The machines focused on one vocal point and that was that John, Sarah Evans' son would be instrumental in shutting them down. Their security service clicked on to New York, off to New York, on to Los Angeles, off and reactivated. The service feed off the night and it was self protection. It's enemies just blinked out and never came back. Arnold was located in Florida. He took over a wildlife sanctuary and became the water moccasin of Male that was dominant. He soothed around and loved being a water moccasin. He craved the foods they craved and fit in the pit of water with moss and pond scum. Tony detected him anytime he disappeared. He returned most any time. Randy Cappone picked up everything on trillion trillion USA on the Hotel California and the Running man. He received permission to advance the mafia legally. He recreated the people with advancement and placed them into eternity that was sanctioned by the State and God. Randy's systems were trillions and the mafia superseded time for they were legal and for the United States.

The mechanical 2 immersion was re-entered by the machine of the future. The Sighris left was none. Arnold was in housing, he made it through time through freezer units the United States one trillion ended with the Confederate Army. Arnold lit up the Joker because his output was originally 100%. The Joker was billion in strength and output and controlled crime 100%. The Joker, a black Tarantula created in Gotham by some equivalency to National Geographic Research scientist output that looked like Jack Nicholson playing Joker without makeup was researched to overtake crime. He found out that the research team was illegal and killed them and ate them down to skeletons. Gotham population was 10 times bigger than the United States. The government of Gotham tried prosecuting Joker and he killed them. In second there were 1 trillion, 3 times, he was quick and precise on killing, he could consume a human body whole. Gotham became a dead zone for a spider that had abilities to knock out and kill an army. Usually the spider kingdom was predictable; the midsized stayed in webs and were easily avoided. You almost had to place your finger on fangs and cause the spider to fight. They were on a different level with 8 legs and a web and looked like they came from Hell. Yet they were controllable. Upon buying a Tarantula you could ask the pet shop owner if it was venomous or not, or whether it bit or not. For Randy Cappone, the pet shop owner would be the Joke, a black Widow Killer Venomous spider only if you were against his company and wanted to kill him. He was cleverer in Monticello because the government tried to sync him in and he was a citizen of the United States that like Cindy Crawford more than anything and he felt the country was trying to ruin him.

Rick Adams

The idea and job of the FBI was to process crime out. The president was their boss. Upon going to Monticello, President George Bush met in warfare technique. Cindy Crawford was frozen, the mafia was frozen. Randy was at every convention and every meeting. The president did not know that he was there. He called him female names. Randy stated that it was not true. He asked the tax department and the State department if he could kill the president. He told the president that he was not going to ruin him. Cindy stated that Randy could remarry just don't go against her. George met and stated "I'm after you, that you beat your wife". He state that he wanted everything of yours dead. He was the worst enemy Randy had. Randy was against him zero. He took over everything of the president's and turned it into the State department. The takeovers were 2 million. Cindy came back after 2 ½ years. Randy worked processes through to transport through in time. He processed gunships through time that were worth trillions and dropped them down in 25 cities that were overtakes for the confederate Army. The Sicilian Mafia had crime since the 1928 and kept it 100% under the Dons' that were criminals. The head of the Sicilian Mafia was Al Cappone. How he lived was, Hoover died by poison at age 80 and Al was 23.

Waco was guns that was legal, the FBI was illegal and killed by John Contii. Because they wanted the family ties of the mafia killed. Earlier Charles Manson signed in the government that he would like to spar with Sharon Tate on the president sublime live, that only Randy Cappone years later go through 100%. He met Cindy, because the military sent her in Lexington to Eastern State. Sharon Tate stated that she wanted Al Cappone's son dead, and a couple of years later in front of the police, Charles Manson, the foreigner Cambodian born that learned the language of American English by soap operas on TV, placed a knife through Sharon Tate's skull because she stuck Charles on government aid and he wanted people to think he supported himself in America. Sharon had the kid earlier. She stated that Charles Manson was the dad. An Irish neighbor named Louis Bates was the dad. The kid went up for adoption. The kid was Italian-Irish. The adoptive parent thought incorrectly that the kid was Charles Manson's. Sara Evans was a factory worker from Los Angeles. She raised her son John through scholastic to be an ace in military and leadership. Arnold watched him at school. The reason he used binoculars was he found John's teacher Tina pretty. She was not of Arnold's classification, an American with dark eyes, a shaped female, a very precise make up and atonement was not in classification for the military. Arnold found her intriguing. John had high grades and would sign up for the military when he was of age, and continue his education and career in the military.

Randy's team were A to Z, the best. He used Indiana Jones technology through the future of States. He cross matched for example Indiana Jones cross matched to accomplishment in National Geographic travel, from his apartment in the fairgrounds. Travel through caverns of computer creativity took Randy and the mafia to Washington quick. There were gun ships and worm holes, etc that took him to the Estates of Cappone. The computer cross matched Indiana Jones to the equal and hid the mafia's position 100%. States worked from apartment 8 and fairground to drop his existence from time. George Bush wanted everything of his deceased. Randy stated you are not going to ruin me. The charges were none at the end of George Bush's presidency and the inauguration of Barrack Obama. The Sicilian mafia of Randy Cappone's had one trillion employees and the organization had more output. Randy was the biggest racketeer ever and went beyond the star system with legal product. Cindy came back one year later and things ran better.

The Administration of Cappone

Arnold was taken over by the Joker and existed no more. Al Cappone and the mafia from the 1920's moved to Alabama and the South. Randy reordered and trained a new mafia. He wheeled out his kids and spoke to Cindy who lived in Hawaii, he liked her and saw her often times, he gained through the administrations. He was legal and went against no one unless they went against him. He was accurate 100%. From Lexington Eastern State to the Confederate Army in Albany, Kentucky, to the FBI in Monticello and the Bush administration, he was prudent with the mafia and gained with a higher output. His Estates was trillions. His name was Randy Cappone, Al Cappone's son. The head Don of the Sicilian mafia and he was legalized in the United States. The location was the state park between Albany, Kentucky and Jamestown. The cave was on level 2 and signified a cave except it was clean and F2 was 100.

Rick Adams

Rick Adams, Randy Cappone inquired was taken out of freezer units. My name's Randy Cappone. The two men shook hands. "Rick Adams is my name. I am an actor from States. I played the Eagle. I scanned States for predators against the country. The movies cross match to locations that they are affiliated to in the movies. When States hit, it evaporated and takes on meaning of the new location. The eagle would cross affiliate to metropolitan areas. The reason we were productive was because our country was founded on zoos that contaminated the location. They were predators that absorbed the environment and became them. We hired programmers and construction companies to save us form the zoos. We were chronic. I played the Eagle, Spiderman and a host of movies hat documented education and means of escape". "Would you like something to eat?" Randy asked. "Definitely". They ate roast beef and Swiss cheese croissants with sour cream potato chips, cottage cheese and root beer. "I am an actor and an escape artist. I can lead an organization to freedom" said Rick Adams. "You're hired" stated Randy Cappone. "Your organization is the Italian mafia. Make certain we get out.". "Most definitely we will or my name is not Rick Adams". The car took them form level 2 to 1. "A bit of an escape artist yourself Randy" Rick stated. "During the Confederate Army systems were developed for the United States. Usually we meet the Confederate Army at their locations from the south to New York. The government people and crime out they were processing the country when the Confederate Army too over. They were deadly. We met them with a gun ship and weapons. We processed the country back the Confederate Army was end of time forces. They were warfare A to Z. They had the equivalent to end time"

During the Bush administration, 9 star systems came in from trillions of years in the future. They were documented to go criminal against the United States and lived. They could repopulate the planet in seconds. Their computers were far progressed into the future. They lasted about a year and a half. Randy rebuilt the mafia to millions and they were placed back where they came from. They said they wanted tax money and Cappone's movies. States A to Z provided education that was beyond recall, an advanced system to utilize output and train employees in all fields. The actors were educated. The State was very educated, crime existed no more. Education was like an addiction or a drug output on the job was outstanding. The mountain, an equal to the rainforest was overloaded with no bugs. Communication was 100%, come on-line fully clothed. Randy Cappone bought it back from the United States president and utilized through a future phone company. It existed in your mind and progressed into a communication. Randy made it a communication that carried 100%. Cindy Crawford made it back and they were inseparable. Randy found it when he recalled the mafia and found that they used Al Cappone, the location came and went trillions of years ago. Randy opened a recreation of him and Al, his dad. They liked him because he worked when he didn't work. The Bush administration was back and President Obama was president. States was set up with recreation they live in dream stages. They live fed by the computer. How States was taken over was by mistake. The recreation recreated a burnt out star system that incorporated the early programs and the ZOOS of prehistoric time dissolved every thing including the burnt out star system. The ZOOS starved in 30 days. States civilization existed no more. States was a complete recall on F2. It was a family level designed to keep Randy's family safe. Cindy Crawford, the super model that had Randy's son. Colt, Cris Perry Brannon's mom was at this level. This level prevented hostage situations. It worked 100% of the time. States was recalled and assessed. Al Cappone's recreation was bought out and systems were their past, present and future of locations and travel. Randy was recreated and took over an automatic service of himself and dropped the systems. Rick Adams played characters such as Venom, a comic came out in bubble gum comics from States. Rick sold Randy Cappone, a package and he A to Z it to the United States in Batman, Spiderman and Superman. He took Rick Adams with permission from Rick Adams and cross-matched him in New York as a man cast of the movies for child molesting. In the 1920's Randy picked up systems from the 1920 director. It worked well for Randy Cappone. The system took him from the FBI coming down from Washington and defeat for the Washington detectives with no charges that tied wedding out crime. The Confederate Army overtake to Monticello and the Bush administration. He picked up the classics and improved the movies 100% and breathed new life by rewriting older serious and movies such as *MASH*, *Indiana Jones* and *Escape from New York*. The movies were A to Z recreated fiction entertainment. He wond all the awards in film and paid the actors and went into economics.

He and Cindy synced. He thought of her as Ultamate Mystace, that was based on romance that took them from life on into life, their connection was good.

Monticello was in reality and fiction in appearance Saturn and 9 planets to be complete in 2 million locations of time and wanted to inhabit the United States for the citizens and abstract the Cappones out of time. The Middle East came in through Cuba and Columbia. The war lasted 2 ½ years and Randy did well. He lived in Albany and Cindy lived in Hawaii. He did well at an apartment and lost nothing, yet gained.

The Steak house burnt and Randy Cappone was 17. He was at home when hell broke open. He and his family lived out in the country five miles. Hell moved in criminal intent. He burnt the restaurant. Lucifer said "You're out in 2". "Two?" Al Cappone said. "Why not 3? You can't take him out with a military beam. As you have to beam them from birth and that fails if you don't beam at birth. It scares them if you process them out with a beam." It was believe the beam was started for fires and floods form the ocean. It was a transport designed for placing United State citizen in pens underground and processing money to the president and through the tax department back to the banks. The FBI crossed 2 million other locations in as doubles and took over the United States until the money was processed back. The government wanted to weed out organized crime. The criminal was the president that kidnapped the United States with no charges and the FBI and military. Saturn under the nine planets killed restaurant entrepreneurs because they modified Christianity to show that Satanism won. Saturn was future and the races were the same as the United States. They were frozen one day, one trillion years. Their job was to let the United States citizens that they could not back anything in their lives and they could take them at anything. The end of regamacy that 2 million locations of time digital trillions into the future would process the United States to the president, the military and the FBI illegally and process money. The locations wanted their kids to have what your kids had and the cross match matched kids that looked like yours to take their places while they starved your kids and processed money. Randy Cappone developed F2 so the citizens of the United States would go there instead of being processed and starved underground. He stole nothing form the country instead he sold product. He was triple A for the country when he went to Monticello, the president George Bush tried processing the country. Randy froze the United States and took out the illegals of the president Bush, the FBI, the military and Bush's state department. He was exceptionally good with Saturn, Utaliptious and 2 million locations. He placed the kids up for adoption and restored them. He literally took their planets in and processed them into the United States government and processed the United States through the tax department. Thus he brought the United States back and George Bush was out of office. The tax department processed George Bush's money back for Randy Cappone and the mafia that was over a trillion, there was no charges. Mr. Obama, our first Black president was aggravated Randy Cappone kept his title of the military, the FBI and processed the tax department's money into the United States for better education, schools, treatment and medical. It was the first time in history that the tax money was processed into the State legally. Randy brought Al Cappone back and the Sicilian mafia established in 1920. Then Cindy Crawford, his wife. Movie sales were high and product that was like a "to go" window. After a sale, the computer would make it days or a day. The service would thank you and go. Pay was important only the company wanted pay only. The reason for illegals from the president was he just wanted to. The rest of the computers were legal and shipped out for the Diamond Computer Company. Diamond was legal into the future for present time computers. On a level undetectable, a sub level computer was disturbed and approved by the government. Usually the computer companies were distributing State approved as on a surface level. Diamond computers did. The companies rarely went to illegals because the State was on their side as to the distribution and there was no fines. Illegal sales could lead to shutdowns, fines or penalization from the court systems.

The United States government was educated in their classification and stated it within every state office being filled with someone qualified, educated and dedicated. NASA was very progressive at making it to other planets through radar. The teams investigated inhabitants of a location that inhibited time differently. The days in America were usually bland and slow moving. School systems provided very little drama and lots of sitting, learning, discipline and output work was output without drama. Most of the time life moved like plowing, uneventfully. We ate the meals we needed, worked the hours to feed and clothe ourselves. Our output was according to our own workmanship and was usually 8 hours a day. A work ethic developed by the State for work ethics and output of legal money. The State Ethic designed minimum wage to know payment and that we legal as United States citizens should have a work ethic that's constitutionally correct in the United States based on morals and workmanship with pay. The movies were rated high in drama A1 with the beginning, ending and middle written and though through. Drama in the average day was a snail's pace similar to plow time. With input on workmanship, the average IQ was based median according to development in school and the training for the environment you lived in. The education training the education training election of public officials were directed to opposition to our military, The FBI was to absorb crime for the president. Our country showed a lack of security in warfare upon President Lincoln being shot, John F. Kennedy losing his life and the impeachment of President Richard Nixon. The President's agenda was supposed to be beyond approach with morals and be protected by the military and State department. The wars that went on the capability of keeping the foreign enemy away and organized crime down. Usually Americans deviated form state protocol early because the regulations for food service, treatment and hospitalizations were designed smart such as the seat belt law to keep you form going through the windshield. The laws were regulated and State employees were in control of certain detail and the police backed it. The protocols were designed to keep America safer and upgrade security.

Egypt

Egypt was a Middle Eastern country that was very future and considered to be the City of the Angels and was a neutral center for the angels to help mankind. The city was very future and had symbols for hairstyles, etc. The angels were spiritual or in spirits in the beginning. Later the angels would receive bodies. The problem was the angels invited devils below, that had been cast down. The supervisor of the team was very quick to point out the fact that the batch had been contaminated and to cast the devils down. He could have dissipated the team when devils flew around. Instead, he let them and the planet survived. He thought that they showed output in other eras. Egypt incorporated with leadership and Pharaoh's. The name translated to Biblical. The output was the slaves were out by a leader of God. The slaves were defiant and tried a new Religion. Law was past and the leader Moses, was defiant and did not see the land that was promised to them. The Egyptians could not pursue because the Red Sea and the Dead Sea blocked them. The Egyptians today were concerned by product and distribution was most of the Middle East after product made it, however it made it. The Middle East went back to business and had no qualms with the United States. The Egyptians were a cross between devils and angels. The races were documented. The country was very progressed, enough to settle issues well within their own communities. The fallacy of many, was that competitiveness was not with people over religion, because the war cold be equalized with guns or physical strength. The United States had protection by the police force. They weeded out and prosecuted crime and illegalities. Compatibility with God and Satan was sin only. Foreign countries were known to be old and trade canal in output. They were prepared for war. The United States, high after product was received there was no need for war and the Middle East returned to normal. The Egyptians were a race of differnental and was a country that made it through time and existed in the Middle East. The animal kingdom was becoming a physical human with a thinking mind was fiction and Lexington, KY left no traces alive in Lexington and the FBI overtake to illegally sync Randy Cappone into the government failed and alive was zero. The rattlesnake tribe from Africa's zoos and wildlife cross matched with thinking mechanism. Randy was surrounded by thinking mechanisms of a killer tribe that never showed up in time. The tribes were spoken of as tribes of Africa. The animals from zoos, having a physical embodiment with animalistic instincts to process food and hunt for food that was alive. One idea was cows dead and half eaten, the lair of a wolf that stood up and killed with claws and dropped out of sight into the bushes and was seen from no more. The stimuli of Halloween and costumes and the superstition that bound use of a fine line. The Sicilian mafia was shadows that backed crime 100%. The Dons incorporated one trillion soldiers that killed. They were Italians, not devils. Their military expertise was high. They dealt in illegals and protected the Don's interests. Their first interest and the founder in the crime organization was Al Cappone stopping the State Department from processing his money out and killing him. Today, his son, Randy Cappone had one trillion trillion men and one Don in all States. It was a big military that protected the Cappone's assets. The wills of Randy Cappone was out, the businesses were legal, the estate set. Randy made trillions on-line. Randy Cappone, a legal service that provided atone time, foods, supermarkets car service and superstores that provided product of all varieties Movies were shown, right in your house. Randy bought the classics from the silent movie to series on TV. He went to a studio after he rewrote movies through that showed years or weeks. There was a service that was the presidents communication on a level of computer stores that picked up on the president's signals almost a telepathic level. The point was the computers existed to carry his orders through time, when he stated on, the military responded. Randy bought this future system from the president and he futurized glasses that were undetectable on into a computer and played movies. He called the communication, The Running man. It centralized the United States in communications and movies played and were offered on –line. Randy Cappone live in an apartment under the fair grounds.

Lexington, Kentucky was a differential beyond any zone. Randy Cappone and Cindy were beyond time and near death from the FBI. A surprise for the president's force against crime was that Randy Cappone worked for John Conti's coffee. He lived in Louisville and waited on John Conti and was dead tired. The manager was upset because the location was not set up and vented anger. John Conti started his order and a fresh cup of Brazilian Santos made it after the selection was brewed and made by Jacky. She was a pretty Irish woman. The coffee selection was made after the mafia Don John Conti ordered. Jacky was angry that the place was not set up and vented her anger.

The moose mall was 2 levels. There was a food court, Baskin-Robbins Ice Cream, clothing stores and burger places. Randy forgot to turn the order in and asked the cook to prepare a chicken salad sandwich quick. The cook was Mark Lyons, a solider for Al Cappone's 1928 mafia. He smiled a charming smile. He was a very good looking Italian. He smiled and said, "I like Randy", and did most of his life. The chicken salad came out fast. He would have told Randy Cappone that went by the name of Randy Cappone that he would be John Conti's boss, he would have been correct. John Conti had one trillion solider and ran drugs. His output for the mafia was 100%. John Conti was happy. When he left Randy was a zero. When he came into work and below zero after the order. Upon leaving, he ordered a pound of Brazilian coffee to go. He ate the order because John Conti was the boss. Later he discovered a lot of bosses of the original Sicilian mafia. The order went through.

Eastern State was Kentucky's psychiatric hospital for shock treatment. The staff was dedicated to following the FBI with a lethal injection into Randy Cappone's veins shutting his system down 100% and killing him. He broke into the main computer and overtook the military's central computer and obtaining weapons. The staff was deceased.

Cindy Crawford helped. She was generated straight in and back. The criminal law of FBI and some kind of Black sin had a cup, a to go cup of poisoning in an underground world to be swallowed by the super model. The rattle snake kingdom was the most unbelievable venomous organization in creation. The devils showed up in papers, big beyond belief and vipers you could say and people did that you could tell that the snake was poisonous by the shape of its head. The rattlesnake, it seemed in diamondback in timber and all forms smelled like skin that the snake molted out of. The point was you saw them dead and Spiders of Black and Gold and a variety of colors were seen in pet shops and in webs. Humans knew the terrain of where to find the anaconda. However was their locations where these predators were as dictative as we humans were. The writer is for people living everyone's endurance is 0-100. It goes no higher than 100 if weaponry was only used for protection by the police force that was for the country. Yet the predators seemed apparent in the zoo. Usually fish and wildlife controlled them. Yet it showed a tarantula eating a bird, the half eaten cattle could have been eaten by dog. Other locations of time showed up with in Biblical turns, Sodom and Gomorrah, that evil, beyond evil bread. The rattlesnakes were the worst tribe of Satan, the devil went through time unnoticed and gained that they were lethal killers that could look human and kill the snakes. The snakes killed deadly and presented an overtake for Randy and Cindy while Randy was at the psychiatric hospital of Eastern State. What started as a trip to Lexington by a deputy and Kentucky State Police, because Randy was at home when a Ouija or a voodoo environment overtook. He walked into town to avoid it. He caught a ride with at waitress and went out to family members' house. His psyche had a hard time processing it. It was a program that was demonstrated by a State department that processed the mind to behave well in the state. The environment was contradictive to education and productivity for its inconsistency could not be explained. Psychotic could vary with change of habit and the availability to not accept something. When the habit is changed and processes are different, you process poorly. The city of Lexington and the state hospital carried a lot of dealings output. Randy's stamina was supported with workmanship from restaurants that was a family business. He was paid 86% where he deserved 90% and had an output of 100%.

Upon moving to Monticello soon after Cindy Crawford was frozen, president George bush communicated war on stage that was considered FBI a magazine circulated prizes were given and the police arrested mobsters upon showing to receive the package. The packages was wigs and fun for staged games 3 to play, you sign and the government tested your skills. John Conti, mafia Don Al Cappone, showed up. He was from The Try It Again, You Stink!, show where when you showed no talent the audience held their noses and said "You Stink, You Stink You Stink!!" The host told the Dons to sign and the paper held by a clipboard stated stage games 3, the host Pat Markum had curly hair and assumed that the police one million, was on active duty would arrest the Don's. the Don's left the talk show. The host was deceased. They used everything that was given to them and looked like 100% alive of the stage games 3 was zero. The magazine stated that the mobsters were arrested.

President George Bush presented himself on Randy's communications and stated that he was a wife beater and that he was on government aid. Randy made certain that any lay off pay or medical insurance was paid back. His money was distributed. He gave Wendy's back to the state. The food was soy in the meat, real meat processed up set stomach and Hardees. His profit was 7 million. He ask an office if Wendy's was advertised pure and an officer stated yes and he stated that he would eat there then. He then stated he would check out his business of Taco Bell. It was advertised on-line that it was soy and was a delicious burger, real meat contained larva and upset the stomach, sales went up.

The teams placed together by Randy was fast effective and had output 100%. Cindy synced well as a super model. The two meet in Lexington. They tried to poison Cindy two weeks before she met Randy and when Randy was in Eastern State in Lexington, they tried poison twice. He had Smith and Wesson.44 caliber sub-machine gun pistols that worked by pick shot it killed one by one or at random. The poison never made it, the bodies dissipated in thin air. Randy came out of the solitude room and sent for bad behavior and a shot usually to calm you down. This time permanently. He came out of solitude to find a new staff. His link of communication with Cindy after meeting her at the Hyatt was far advanced into the future. He activated it with an eye print and contacted her by visual 100% of the time 100% accurately. After Lexington, Randy stayed at the Hope Center for a year, a homeless shelter. The charges by the FBI in Albany was he needed to synch into authority that he lived in Louisville and after work they stated he did what he wanted and should have more authority. Cindy Crawford was always were she was supposed to be, in Los Angeles. She was a very expensive super model. The spontaneous of the eye retinal, the shadows appeared in group therapy. It paid if you were honest. The shadows were a society that took over trillions and trillions of years ago, at the dawn of creation. The science or engineering department listed the last world. It was common and mentioned was the biggest criminal of all time. He was entered in the Night Stalker. Richard Adams honestly stated he was dried up and had no access to time. He took time and went away on a web. He played Batman kids characters at Halloween or the equal t in costume for another time. He killed everything he ever met and became them. Government games, meant he got to eat. He ruled all time. He was in Batman, Spiderman and Superman. It showed because no human could get around like that unexplainable before, only the men of Crime Prevention got around, he explained. He was the most evil ever, a Black Widow that didn't die during mating. He died of lack of ovadation. He lived trillions of years ago and lived beyond time. When he died galaxies ended and a new one had to be started. He was the biggest predator ever created, was true when he spoke before the planet Earth today, it was the same states went A to Z beyond comprehension crafted educated well. The zoos were coded in against the take over of a burnt out star system serpents made political sport of states men and women. Al Cappone conditioned the computer to overtake states. Al was entered into the computer of states prehistoric and systems were re-modified. Randy Cappone recalled all systems of Al's trillions of years after states he gave Al his systems 100%. States came through and invited Randy back.

The night clubs were Coyote Ugly, the manager cross matched the movie and had an escort service. The club highlighted the belly button as bartenders. The ladies were thin and accentuated sex. The escort service with office in the back, was expensive. The women were signed out and checked back in. Rob Lowe owned Poison Sex Toys, the Black Widow Inn and he owned a Marvel comic book store. He loved comics and went to Marvel when new comics came in. He chewed bubble gum and wore a baseball cap. He looked like tom Cruise. The other night club escort service was Jesse James' Outlaw Club. He dressed well and killed for pleasure, just like his career was killed. He killed at his service rarely. Randy Cappone bought Playboy. He though of nudie magazines as equate to males of the female bodies degrade came on actions and parents and friends viewing them. There was guys that got married and did not know the female body and took their wives to the hospital thinking they were wounded. He owned Hawaiian Tropic and hundred of agencies, his wife was Cindy Crawford and was the best built. He killed women only if they tried killing his family. Saturn a planet that registered in our society, unproven, tried taking over the Cappone's and their kids. They wanted the United States, hook, line and sinker. He placed their kids up for adoptions and they were the same race as the United States. Rob Lowe heard people speak bad about him, rarely when he got defensive, was when they found his house and tried to extract him from time. They were mostly females after him because he was extremely good looking. The extra good looking wanted to tie him up and extract his life in a dozen of sexual ways. These ladies tried to get their men to beat him up. He found their names out and the Venomous ones, he abducted in sexual conques. He felt that they died happy. Rob went by the name on his ID in business and rarely did they recognize him. His IQ was high and his killer instincts were primed. Usually he called the police on the destructive males. He defeated them one way or another. He was innocent of his charges of child pornography. States A to Z, he opened it his recreation and made certain that he could not be recreated through time. He had a life time of accomplishments. He place in his programmed computer and he re-wrote it though he did movies and other things. Rick Adams was classified an ace. He worked for Randy and edited the administration out of the Sicilian mafia. Randy connected with him after Spiderman was released. He was edited into another Spiderman. Randy had the right to Spiderman from marvel comics and bought the movie rights. He picked Spiderman. The one he wrote though, was based in Los Angeles. He played an officer. Spiderman was the actor on Silk Stockings. Cindy Crawford played Angela. Spiderman was an officer of the law that took vengeance against crime.

Rick was dropped when Randy played the director and picked the second Spiderman up. He cross matched it to directors during the Twenties and was the one that dropped the systems. Rick Adams was finished before he started. Randy went to states and cross matched Spiderman, a Marvel comic with states equal and progressed the estates of Cappone. The character of the movies and the actors reached beyond the future for Randy Cappone. He created the effects of a movie that moved into two million other locations of time. One was called Exon. The movie and effects was dramatized criminal studio. A door opened as of waling into a movie theater and effects of movies created, opened. It had effects that was high and travel to two million locations that went trillions into the future compared to the U. S. present time. The effects brought the movies to life and you could become a character in the movies. The program took you to locations never charted in the United States. Saturn and 9 planets sent information of their existence and charted themselves. We made it there none, they made it here 100%. The other locations were not charted. The 9 planets were a complete take over. The mafia minded their manners in this location and traded goods.

Bob Brown

The business suite was defended well and accentuated. The name on the ID was Bob Brown, his hair was gray. He was very distinguished. On his way out of Bailey's, a very seasoned and expensive diner, the staff was stated chocolate; they smiled and said were black. The owner, Chaz Bailey, was white. He ordered packages and kept the reorder expensive. The uniforms were expensive, the food was seasoned. The black staff was AAA good looking. He had seasoned Cajun autumn festivities and a rich cup of Vanilla Cream Latte. A young lady of 23 built AAA introduce herself as July Roberts. July, because she liked explosives in time. Bob helped push her Rolls Royce off the pavement. She called for a pick up. Bob Brown gave her a ride. "Do you work out or anything?" Bob asked. Her chest was pert. She was extremely thin and very good looking. She smiled. "I know this freak that I ran by his house. He has a daughter that he molested. I would love to kill him." "You are angry. Why so angry? I didn't think that you would kill" He offered her his drink. The only reason was to keep her energy level up so he could have her sexually. "I would have you if you would have me." Bob took her to a hotel room and they had sex. She state in bed that even 30 years later she would love to conquest Rob Lowe in bed and waste him because of child pornography. "You never know about actors and fiction" Brown stated. "I'd like to blow him away" she smiled. She was made up well and very accentuated as a female. There was a gleam and the sharp knife penetrated her heart. His brown eyes turned to snake. "You're him!" she stated. She died. One of a gang that caused him to move was out for good. He had to move because they destroyed his residency by telling the neighbors about him. They broke into his house and spray painted "Child Pornography King". Their boyfriends followed the organization fully into death. Rob Lowe's name was entered into death sequels hundreds of time. Most had worn off because his career ended a long time ago. Mr. Brown or Rob Lowe, who dyed his hair gray, turned his key in. "Thank you Mr. Adams." He gunned his car and made it to another location. He dyed his hair black and changed clothes. He looked noting like Bob Brown. He wore jeans and his hair was dark brown. He left the rental car outside of town and had another car. He drove back to the hotel. The police took the body out. He looked completely different. She was taken out dead on a stretcher. A neighbor, Mary Abberson, stated to the police, "She was a good girl. The only person she hated was Rob Lowe". She broke down. He looked concerned. She thanked him, "The reason she hated him was because well it wasn't because of child pornography It was because July knew his daughter and she told her that he was really nice and a master at cunning. She stated that he was lite and she would love to see him dead because he could not back villains and if he were smart he would have cured the charges of child pornography. She stated that he couldn't back his life." Her body was placed in the ambulance. Rob Lowe got in his car and drove off.

Her name was Laura. She was a god friend of Billy Ray Cyrus. She went to his house with colorful cupcakes that she baked. They melted in your mouth and were as colorful as Halloween or Easter. She said that like Peg on Al Bundy's "Married with Children, she wanted him to put on weight. He smiled and placed a cupcake above his head like a baby boy and ate a piece. The chocolate almond cupcake melted in his mouth. She stated Peg had a work out professor for a couple of weeks and she fattened him up. He smiled and said, she was like a sister and he didn't eat that much. "Eat one" he stated, smiling. She was a double A, very pretty. Her build was good. The two meet at a part and on in to S. A., (Sexual Anonymous). The reason was the town didn't know each other and in the middle of winter they lost a bet and had to hug each other in their skivvies. His underwear was cruddy because he was at a neighbor's house and sat where the baby was changed. He knew nothing of it. She was built well, his build was good and they were out in the cold. They had to hug for five minutes. She was cold, both were shriveled up. The police came and arrested them. A picture was taken. The Birmingham Alabama newspaper presented it as moral deficient. They were held five minutes. The judge stated five meeting of S. A. The meeting chairman stated, no dating and Laura and Billy Ray Cyrus agreed to be friends. Billy was into fantasy for a price. He made money from women for romance. He made money and when a profit was in, he produced rooms, expensive with exotic fountains and plush from landscapes, Hawaiian gardens and expensive environments. That was very pleasing. He had cameras that were expensive and was sold expensively, that showed everything but the exchange of money. She took the tape with her. He edited out most mistakes and usually they left happy. He brought cities to life with glistening snow. The cities were 1800 Boston with a fireplace and all of the advantages of early time and the food matched the time. I was good for a weekend. The world was reentered at the end. Billy had 10 worlds that were very realistic. He was very cleaver and educated at his job of romance and was paid well. Laura traveled around a lot. She liked guys well when she dominated. She had a lot of money because she bought businesses and sold them within a couple of days. She knew the price from the book. She bought them from Real Estate and sold them to businessmen. She met guys that loved to be tied down and to have female underwear place on them. She was a sex package beyond belief. Her charisma was high. She respected people that were straight and behaved well sexually. When they were dominated and followed her around, she detested it. She received a call from Louis Flemming. "Hi Laura. I'm wearing them women's lingerie. They fit well". "Louis, we broke up. Leave me alone" He called in a raspy voice and said he was going to rape her. He showed up with colorful cakes in clown outfits. The cakes state Happy Birthday Laura. He gave her colorful balloons and played a mime. She held a gun in a parking garage when some one looking like Gene Simmons from KISS followed her in full costume. She was very nervous as she walked to her car. "I have a gun. The night was balmy. A carnival with brilliant colors lit up 25 floors. The smell of popcorn was in the air. She could hear heavy breathing. "Louis, I have a gun." He looked like a young Gene Simmons. "Laura, you were mean to me. I must even the score by leaving a chalk of your imprint." He smiled approaching. "I can smell your vagina". The gun barked. Laura said "Ah!" She looked sensual. The body fell, Laura, the clown's outfit of Gene Simmons lay on the ground. A black dog scurried out, climbed the wall and climbed down the building in a web. He was at Billy Ray Cyrus' home in a second. He looked just like Jack in Batman without the clown makeup. "Laura is on a rape mode. I usually don't care, yet you did some acting for Randy Cappone on the remake of Amanda Condac. The Black Widow tarantula stated he didn't die during mating. "Yes I played a tour guide in Anacondas"

"Laura thinks of herself as independent and believes she can handle herself in any situation with a man. I know that you're Randy Cappone's right hand man. Please tell him The Joker was out through the window non existent" What ate the minds of Rob Lowe and Laura was the demonstration from extremely good looking people to being filed down to nothing. Somehow books were written as a validation for equivalency to regeneration. Billy Ray Cyrus chose clientele carefully and screened them out in variation. They felt that S.A. was weak because sexual started at 12 years of age, puberty for male and female and had an outlet daily and weekly and you were taught behaviors in your mind from 12, minus or add, hygiene and bathroom stops. Rob Lowe was in his office. He owned the club Poisonous Sex Toys, that checked in and out, an escort service. They had dancers, that was popular. He hated them because of sexual experienced in their pants publicly when suggestive women showed ample breast and tight underwear. The proceeds were high. He called them in his office rarely because they were place together well and promoted sex like a variety of your favorite foods.

Randy went into his lifetime one state here, a tape go back to that room. The issuer was homosexual. Randy exited the pasilates and went to a Mexican restaurant and had a margarita. The second time he was with a girl he met at a Greyhound bus station. She wanted a drink. The dancer performed for him. He gave his attention to the woman he was with, without disrespect. That was before he met Cindy in Lexington. The playboy agency really had a purpose, married or single on condition of sexual and the human body. He owned male magazines and just let them edit through time. His interest was none. The government was strange about the Sicilian mafia. Randy was legal, all of his companies were legal. There were 2 million companies the government tried with charges on companies that were legal and there wasn't any charges. They knew that Al transgressed through time and made his money legal by robbing people that tried for his money in tax evasion.

Cindy was fabulous as a super model, her pay was high. Randy picked up super models 100%. The endorsement went high with million of supermodels endorsing product and restaurant internationally. Poisonous Sex Toys lit up Los Angeles, New York and Miami. People had ultimate sexual and needed it the next night. It was reoccurring daily. There were politicians, ministers, etc. that got real far out with prostitution and wound up in the papers. Prostitution was illegal and usually the police shut both down. There were no government laws on cheating, morals were broken and wives would divorce yet he almost had to turn himself in and she would not have been endorsed by the police. Most men would not cheat because they married who they wanted to be with and stayed with them if they wanted to be with someone else they broke up first. It was smarter and cleaner. Randy played Tony Montana for about ten years. During the Confederate Army overtake President Clinton started selling drugs and he sold them because the president stated the country needed drugs. The mafia controlled the drug trade. It was a compliment. Some of the moralistic that enjoyed the drugs, they dealt to churches 100% of America that was

21. He got high Seldom when he moved to Monticello, he entered the drugs into a cigarette. He posted the Surgeon General's warning for lung cancer. The United States did well against the Confederate Army. President Clinton dropped the United States underground, with a future military strategy. Before he signed for warfare with the head general of the Confederate Army an army that could not be proven to exist, the south repeated one million one hundred times and joined the Confederacy 100%. They were picked up, their mission was to end time.

Rick Adams saw Poisonous Sex Toys flash to life from his apartment overlooking the sky, during Monticello; his programmer hooked Randy Cappone up to a virtual reality program that made him a master of disguise. His output Cindy played. She played a second editing of "Back to the Future". Randy played Michael J. Fox's Mary McFly. An unknown played Michaels replacement girlfriend. Her name was Larenzo. She played the unrecognized character. When Randy played Rick Adams, he was unrecognizable and stationed in New York by a star system beyond ideas I the future for them, it was present time. This location populated by future travel, during the moon travel of the Untied States, the documentation of travel was limited because nothing was brought back to prove that the United States made it to the moon and there was no real proof of the 9 planets orbiting the planet earth. Computers were shown on TV before color was added they showed real, too real. The news showed during the Olympics, that Adolph scoffed blacks, yet he was an illegal dictator that took over dozens of countries because the tax department broke him down from his form. He lost nothing in his life. He took over the military. He took over the United States and dropped it mechanically and the only computers that showed was real reel to reel that took gymnasiums to equal today's. The travel from locations to locations was documented. A language from Science Fiction, the proof of existence had not been proven.

Al Cappone had no memory because Randy picked it up and gave Al all the systems and no memory. Al recreated the Zoos only to go against society when they went against him. He was an educated con. Randy introduced himself on a get away. States welcomed him, their systems were very adequate. The stars brought the conclusions to a day. The theory was trillions of years away, a star brought lit almost like a sun to planets. The actual proof was zero, the moon walks did not seem to improve the status of the United States. You would nee to look at the economy. States used recreation of Al Cappone well adapted to make it through prehistoric overtake Zoos that would decease the location. Besides that the city was civilized. States progressed well. Their computers picked up the biggest con and villain of time past, present and future and incorporated him to over take predators that became them and to keep time going. Al Cappone was recreated by computers bright in. Adolph Hitler was masculine for a German that was taken over by the tax department and hung out to dry. George Bush was frozen for 3 years and Cuba tried as a replacement and 2 million were-dogs that wanted the country to bleed and Randy Cappone, out of commission. All were prejudiced against Blacks and tried for hostile take overs because President Obama was black. With President George Bush back at his ranch house and his term complete, the United States was returned to normal and the public returned from units that passed them as doubles took them over. Time returned to normal. Cindy Crawford returned and she and Randy were reunited and inseparable. She acquired more years by sinking in underground and being frozen by the United States. She was very young. The marriage to Richard Gere was annulled.

Randy had outputs on teams through the movies. Indiana Jones synced well and increased output for Randy and the mafia. Randy Cappone On-line synced product through time and sales were high. On-line communications synched your thoughts into vocals and allowed for communication that was clear. It originated with the president and stated on for warfare for the military and the president acquired programmability that melted the mind with heart attacks, breathing deformities and all synched devilish. Ideas such as take overs of yourself by a double, a replay of revolution convincing you that you are the antichrist or the messiah. It prompted prayer was stated, in fact it caused mental instability and hospitalizations. Randy Cappone created IBM that ran through the government mind. He placed himself on the program and society. It worked. Thus he kept society on it and developed other options. The new president integrated protocols 3 and activated it upon his inauguration. I. B. B. was for a public that worked it well against the Confederate army. In Monticello, Hillcrest, the overtake was Saturn and 9 planetary systems. These Civilizations were not ended by the Confederate Army, because they served Satan and went against the Untied States on criminal charges. The Untied States ended on the take over number one. Saturn was placed in freezer units and time resumed on a remake one million and one hundred United States. The overtake of Saturn was trillions of future years. The sexual outlet of Kink Clubs did fair. Rob Lowe retaliated for false charges by absorbing other locations and killing a prostitute. Casey was in and out of sleeze, mostly out. Randy, who picked up Playboy and incorporated bunnies as a team. Sexual killings were rare because sex was supposed to be pleasurable. Sleeze magazines had a place to show what the human body looked like. Thus upon dating or marriage, adults were not surprised of sexual organs.

Randy was at an apartment in Albany that he rented, talking to Cindy in Hawaii. His phone was visual. He spoke of a lost world, centuries ago. A call came in on a third line, "Hi Randy", Cindy was mute with visuals and sound. "Hi, I am Stephanie, a school teacher from the land of Aquarius, the location came and went centuries ago. The location was bought from the city of the Angels, Egypt. The package went to Black Widow Tarantulas from 20 mile south in the country. They received future packages and opened a city for them to live in the program. They held packages to be in human form. One hung form a web in a bedroom, one was male, and the other took on a pharaoh with a shaven head. The one that looked like a pharaoh watched the city. There was a million of them concentrated in the city and fed rodent food. When phone calls came through Aquarius, the city of trillions, laughed in that general era at the spiders that received a package from Egypt. The spiders were deadly. They thought light in Aquarius' people went out to the country of Egypt and tried opening doors.

Jake Flanders

The spider community became venomous and killed then they ejected their skeletons outside. Science was at work. Jake Flanders, from Aquarius came up with a research that would make him Hercules. He used on his breakfast and he gained little weight and little mass. He was at work in a forest area and dumped the substance on garbage and the garbage was out in front of the compound. The birds ate the garbage and spiders, the snakes, the flies and the wooded area was dense with predators that were 100 times their size, spider of A to Z variety breed. Snakes were the same. Aquarius forests were grounds for prey. The city was surrounded by a big web. The city was Sullivan. Randy was contacted several trillion years into the future. He got spray in the past and killed off the spider kingdom. He suggested they use military freezer units to make it through time. There were worlds that went into animal species as an original species, such as human frequented the United States. Most of those locations came and went. It was impossible to believe that from the dawn of that location, species of birds and prey ruled. Some locations fed black widow tarantulas. Male dominant, they were used to meet from the zoos When fed meat they started killing humans. They almost made it through time, frozen in freezer units. The beast tarantula lived hundreds of years. When they died, time ended and the whole location was in existence no more. Another planet was started and there was no recall. The animal kingdom being an aspect of human development, was uncharted as nine planets being populated and through the Bush administration coming in to since America's money in by taking them off F2 and processing money in. Seemingly the FBI and military would populate somehow. Cuba made it in and played the administration. They somehow managed to look American and speak American fluently

The animal kingdom was processed through a recreation of eternity and through this process, lived as long as a human. The cobras were very big and the animals took on their last victim that was consumed 100%. They left no sign. Randy Cappone's right hand man was the Joker. He was dominant sexually and was very mafia organized. He was good at executing Randy's orders. He looked like jack playing the Joker with no makeup. His output was 100%. Two million freshly hatched animals took on human form. They knew better. Sodom and Gomorrah was the location. There was no human alive when they hatched out. They took on their last victim, whether it was a cow or a pig. They were remade by the Sicilian mafia for protection from war zones. They were excellent at what they did. They looked precisely like the enemy.

The Bush administration was differently organized because the Confederate Army occurred, Randy Cappone was responsible for trade, the military and government functions. The Bush administration got through nothing, because the Sicilian mafia progressed for the country 100%. Cindy was out for 2 ½ years. Randy picked up super models 100%. The classic movies, any movie released in American and thousands of companies, he re-modified a mafia of one trillion and picked up 2 million women and robbed America back when they tried to steal. What ruined the presidency was they said that he wanted his youngest kid dead, Colt. He computerized the govern-ment down and reprocessed George Bush out. People enjoyed items in America as they wanted. If someone stated whether you liked some thing or not and you hadn't tried it, the person may have personal choice. If nice bout the person that stated the constitution liked you if you truthfully stated your case afterwards your tastes were know in that area. For example, to be popular or not, the men could order a plastic device crudely called a dildo that the male placed on for size enhancement. It was plastic and came in real flesh. In porno, they placed on and were very personified, such as you would be around your friends over sport communications.

The military was educated to this year. The mafia had to reorder and re-focus the military. They remembered the organized network of the 1920's. They thought that they would make certain Al Cappone was legal. The pres-ident was 100% paid for by taxes and the state department from the elections to the ads on TV. It would be well to hire senators and president s with the best being open to the state and all races masculine and feminine and a director to make certain the distribution was cleared by the state department. Randy Cappone distributed free food for the hungry during the Confederate Army overtake and a neutral area to prevent hostage situations. He was 100%. The death toll was zero during the 7 year war. The overtake of the United States and the actual killings took no more than an hour by guns the general sur-rounded each city dead and succeeded 100%. During the 1800's it was war games. The reason president Lincoln was killed was because he was debasing after the war and behaved like he really over took the Confederate army.

Los Angles circulated a book that spoke of political sexual killings. It was run underground and spoke of how to be a predator and win on political sex. The mafia centralized well, yet kept out of investigations. The book allowed that you even 100% Rob Lowe gained from the beginning. The extreme was unusual, yet trained the mind for sexual killing. Normally they would behave differently. Randy Cappone centralized America 100% on F2 with output. President Clinton centralized them underground to look into finances. The teams opened to the Sicilian mafia that contained Irish, Orientals, Blacks and other races. It was called a crime syndicate and reached the United States 100%. All States had a mafia of one trillion. A to Z, the guns prevented over-take of the U.S.A. The teams were astronomical. The output of the Cappones and the Sicilian mafia was depicted by States and the facility of recreation. It went trillions of years in the future. Access to the Stars came from States re-productivity. To escape the Venomous Serpents designed by a star system that came and went. States gave Randy Cappone the future. He was accepted 100%. The forest areas operated well, the computers had time travel access to past Unites States that ended. Seventy worlds that were in existence in this solar system for billions of years. The takeovers were 2 million that included 9 star systems, the modified Satan with the Confederate Army. States was a workable location that succeeded far into time and fielded the present future beyond time. Learning was a nutrient that was enjoyed vested in with outlet beyond dreams. Their survival techniques were beyond belief. Their education and output was very exquisite. Their recall gave Randy Cappone access to one million locations past, present and future that unlocked time.

States and ingenuity took Cappone Estates from A to Z expansive. The systems took Randy to cross matched United States far into the future. The end was the Confederate Army and 9 planets, the total being 2 million locations that came into the Untied States when the president issued the State department kept the presidents communications clear by cross matching the FBI quantum leap that made it seem like the State department went to locations while in their office they stayed. The same for the military. The communications were taken over 98% while America waited and listened. When the president gave the order, America was dropped underground and the president processed a country that was legal and 2 million locations that were not documented existing. They took over through the military. They became America.

Randy sated that his favorite movie was "The Sting" with Robert Redford and Paul Newman. That the importance was some people tried holding on to certain items till you changed them. The mafia took over your game completely when you went against the Italians of the mafia. On their behavior they gained 100% of the time. He was very expensive and trained to overtake the mafia. The mafia played games none of the Sicilian mafia sold legal product highly.

States buried Randy deep into another location, while Cindy was out of commission. Randy went there with a different super mode or actress. The populations of kids went up and grand kids for Al Cappone, Randy paid for them 100%. The mothers raised them and were triple A exquisite super models. Playboy was the only escort service that was legalized in the United States. The Playboy Bunnies were modified triple A. Their output was triple A for the company. The Hawaiian Tropics girls were triple A tanned volleyball sports, etc. however you accentuated work out. The movies existed. Randy placed together, a team from Lord of the Rings by making Stephen King the main actor. He computerized Gotham to get him out and back without casualty. His output was AAA. He formulated programs from programs of the animals getting away 100% of the time. Lord of the Rings was like the young Indiana Jones Chronicles cross matching the young Stephen King, who was an announcer of Horror at the company memo Horror that was announced like Elvira, Mistress of the Dark, he was edited in on Halloween. The actor edited in writes was popular when Halloween was edited out of his horror show, Stephen Spielberg was a repeat. He was a chacoostoo, who announced sharks on National Geographic. He was taken out because he was on the presidents' line on stage in which you agreed to play. Randy Cappone was the only one that contradicted it. The reason the State complied was because they owned the movie rights and believed the president or black market would process them underground. They believed that he could process them out by the military of Satan with 9 planetary systems and the United States was starved until the last turned over bank accounts to the president. Randy developed a level of F2 to keep America from being hostage and legally processed money back. Stephen King was given good packages from a Halloween show with Gilbert Godfrey and was re-edited millions of different times as a writer. Stephen Spielberg's sharks from National Geographic Discovery went into prehistoric times and then park and was edited in director. The cast of the classics were paid government aid and were taught advertisement none the movie went on automatically. The only difference was, Randy re-wrote a re-edited with old and new actors. The same with supermodels.

Tina Marcum

Cindy made a debut and was able to come back. Her debut was called "Forever Cindy" and went to number one. She retired and other supermodels were edited in. Randy owned super modeling 100%. States was an oasis for Randy Cappone. He was told by Cindy that he could have relationships. She stated a "get even" J. R. Ewing style, she stated. She said, "Raise the kids and say nothing about it."

The Monticello Township was a small town. Randy found it cozy. Cindy was in Hawaii. The Estates of Cappone was rich. Randy bought 925 estates. The Bush administration staged wars through time. The Gulf War was Columbia based. The death toll was 1000 Columbians. They tried to smash the twin towers with a plane and succeeded. Randy found the Columbians in Columbia and deceased them within one week. George Bush, the warmonger that he claimed to be, staged the war after Randy settled it. Saddam Hussein, lived after the war and gained.

Cindy was frozen in the Estates and 2 years after the staged Gulf War, George Bush declared war on the Cappones, especially Randy, because Al was frozen for relocation in Monticello. The charges that never made it to the state police was wife beating. Two million FBI came to overtake the Cappones and become Cindy. The bodies were place in the dumpsters. The night was thick with black magic form George Bush's protocol computer was as thick as black oil. It was a form of smoke as much as an extract as a gourmet coffee company's almost clear coffee with very little color, yet an extract of clear loaded in caffeine. The thick black smoke, not traceable, came from Hell. Randy caught every meeting of warfare. The claim was he wanted to give male underwear, Bikini Red a the military called it. It was like a chapter of Bullwinkle and Rocky, yet the military took it seriously and the FBI and the state department. They wanted to process Randy's money over wife beating. He made every meeting in Washington much to George's surprise. Randy had gunships that was stored and transport through time. The charge was wife beating. He stated stages of government aid, Randy's finances were trillions, then looking straight, he place his hand over his mouth and stated Red Bikini, he muttered, and stated "Your wife wants your money and everything of yours dead." President Bush, the politician he was, looked like the fictional character of O'Hara in Star Trek. Randy had on-line communication bugged and knew that it lit up stage. Cindy wants Red Bikinis in Valentine's red. It was supposed to be a surprise that a Randy look a like. He was thoughtful, George looked out. He thought that he was company commander and controlled Randy's fate. Randy looked at him and asked "Are you the one that scrolled out Cindy signed for Red Bikinis and Randy should give Cindy Red Bikinis and his money"? George looked forward and thought he was coy and Randy did not catch it. Stage Randy stated was a ploy of Saturn whether civilization are real or fraud. Saturn was trying to pause time by a standoff between Jehovah and Satan. The location stated they were on Satan's side and 2 million turned nothing in, Saturn came in when the president went against a company to turn the business in to the president. George looked at Randy like an eagle. "I have a military to command and a state department. I want your kids dead." Randy went from 100% to zero, psychotic he could not believe it. "My kids dead?" He dropped George Bush's pants and placed his fist up George's anal passage and robbed the White House. "You never speak of kids being killed in America. He robbed the White House and George went to the hospital.

Steve Baker

Oil was distributed by Randy Cappone. He picked it up, after the remake of "Dallas". Re re-edited another J. R. Ewing, Steve Tate. He was a shoe in for Larry Hagman and had great output. He asked all of the oil well tycoons if they wanted oil. They said they had enough, take it. He modified it 100% from the Middle East to the United States. Randy found the original J. R. Ewing. He was in the movie "Dallas" portrayed by Larry Hagman. He was on world one and there was one million one hundred worlds of U. S. A. J. R. Ewing was oil. He lost on the Black market. Jock, his dad, played Estates games with England. He could not process them through time. He thought that maybe his sons could.

The movies were real life that meant the companies processed drama through the movies. The people that played in drama such as an oil baron, etc. signed and a programmer reprocessed memories through time from an organization that wanted to be in the movies. The books processed in quick dubbing from memories, the actors and editors even the directors were edited in and special effects. The actors that were edited in were paid state. The real life was frozen people. Randy Cappone changed the movies by rewriting them and made a bundle.

States was refreshment. Menthol came from ice and pines. The pine was a refreshing antidote for Randy Cappone. When he went to Monticello, his teeth bled from lack of calcium. I scared him, the apartment was comfortable.

The Cappone organization had trillions of dollars. The Untied States was paid for every company. The only thing the Sicilian mafia owed for was the next bill ordered at a restaurant they did not own. President George Bush was hostile against the leader of the mafia. He spent hours breaking down organizations of warfare and checked the Estates. He found Shania Twain in the Estates and super model agency 1-2-3. He had access to any organization A to Z from F2. He paid them and was legalized by the state and paid the organization 100% and fined only if they went against the company of the Sicilian mafia. The Corelone's were an organization of Sicilian mafia that brutalized Chicago. They ran crime and followed Al Cappone's orders 100%. The mafia was easy to keep up with. Al Cappone started it and the State department want to shut down legal businesses of Al Cappone, the crime family overtook the State department that wanted Al Cappone and his family dead and led with the biggest military of Italians warfare ever. Al had business sense and military warfare techniques. He lost nothing on tax evasion. The Corelone's of the Godfather A to Z, organized crime. The organization was named Sebastian Bach. Bach was the godfather. The organization repeated 3 time s and was Gestapo mafia war soldiers. The mafia was protection for the assets of the Don.

States took Randy to and from tracks of time The United States repeats and locations. Unbelievable. Randy was buried beneath the sea with Jennifer from the Dukes of Hazard. The sea was contained with hidden filters that ozonated and had state parks for seeing fish that was tropical. It was impossible to find and showed no entrance for the existence was on a dream stage. Jennifer conceived of Randy's baby and went to the estates. States hid the Estates of Cappone Rob Lowe interpreted people that his career went because of charges from an angle of perversion because he went on child pornography. He had no sexual for kids and liked kids. The win was with the actor every morning, when he woke up. It would go nowhere in Rob Lowe's life time. He thought of his ruined child pornography night and day. Children were not available for sexual content nor as a several level because our department was differentiated, you are not drunk unless you drink alcohol. We all grew up and knew the behavior of ourselves as children. The state educated us well or poor.

The Hotel California was a theme park designed by the State. It was horror and excitement it sold enticements that were good for the soul. The liquid was high in caffeine and caffeine was out of society. The State department did not know the contents were caffeine and they knew everything. It was drank less because it was black. The Hotel California was a black solution that made your soul feel better. It had more or less caffeine than the other with caffeine. The other had 100. The Hotel California solution with palm tree had 67 percent. The solution sold some. The song was edited through time theme park. The tax evasions and signature was a joke if you singed for communication in America or Satan. They would just say don't serve under communism and make certain there was no outlet. Horror was A to Z wonderful if you liked horror. The Running Man was John Roark. His wife was extremely good looking and helped him lots as a combination, he dropped Sara York maiden name Sarah Roark, his wife. John was a military major that was at home for the weekend when the enemy attacked brutal was John Roark's techniques. He made it to the United State fiction as John Roark, The Survivalist.

States was designed to cross match companies of the United States trillions upon trillions of years into the future of a past world. Randy Cappone picked up every ting 100% and cross matched it to the United States to become a tangible reality and obtained the rights in America. An example was Spiderman that was Venom in States. He obtained permission and bought the rights in both.

Stephen Foster

Stephen Foster was designed military during prehistoric time of States. He was a major in the military that encouraged his sons 1-6 to become educated I the military early. The youngest was 17 and went to Zone protection after fully receiving State education, the process trained in warfare against eh tribes of Venom at food productivity and when War Zones opened, an officer that protected the State was killed by organizations that received very little education and retaliated when sex and child bearing were spoken of. The organizations were very superstitious and when the State department tried to educate, they became angry and self defiant. Those locations had the same access to military and police as other districts, yet their education centers were unused. The populous kept kids at home to work and make output at home. Stephen Foster trained his sons and the Sate Department in the military and police. His wife was very pretty and young. He kept her young by freezer units. He crafted a team and taught them to proceed in all eras. He was for this location and wanted to see it proceed legally. He tried manufacturing most everything into the equivalency to a bomb shelter that was a basement that was constructed by a computer that hid position. Stephen and his family woke up and watched from the basement as prehistoric time was overtaken by low modified people of other eras. They were low modified tribes or organization of teamsters. They modified the legal State of the location called States Back and tried to reprise it.

Stephen Foster was surprised when on leave, he woke up and the location was overtaken over 100 trillion, a thousand times were killed. Prehistoric time States was equal to 2040 time in the United States and the buildings abandoned and the teamsters over took about a billion of the military and police. Stephen Foster froze his 6 boys and 6 girls. All were mated and he and his wife assessed a way to proceed.

Stephen Foster's youngest was Stephen Jr. He promoted with the military and the police department. He was clever abut the people he met. He processed the State Department employees through on education of how to behave at processes that would kill off their exultancy in States. His dad, Stephen Foster was a crack at processing warfare. Stephen was good at negotiations. His youngest wasn't as personalized and cut faster ad better because he wasn't as personalized with the officials at other locations. The admirals were processed that solved things. If product made it and knew qualifications through police work and employees, he stressed importance for States to continue and spoke of pay at 20. Stephen Jr. was capable of employment of State Department employees on a level of emergency and clearance of finical care from the State Department. Stephen Jr. was in the computer recalling records and processed a black widow Tarantula, a male that through recreation became human and processed to eliminate teams that did not comply with the State. The enemy became victims and was reduced to prey quickly. He had the human body of a weight lifter with high output in the muscles. He was trained a specious feed that passed through legal or illegal if not processed through the State with no consequences, could go against Foster, because the State would not be able to process his aggressor out. The tarantula was named Robert Baker. His output in protection and security was one thousand when most security was 63% at the most 100%. Foster Jr. picked the security operative up when Al Cappone was processing the zoos form a burnt out star that processed States through to present day. Foster Jr. picked up employees; he trained them through the State Department and legalized them through the military and police department. He showed up when he froze them in Foster's freezer units and proceeded the family of foster, a military family million s on survival techniques. The rest of the family relied on the military provided by the State and hired by the State. In the State Department, the laws and regulations were made to protect the people of the States location. The police were legalized by the law the military was the same at warfare. The police and military was trained by and educated by the State department to weed out illegals, while remaining legal t the State Department. The police and the military functions were the same.

States prehistoric time went on trillions of years. Volcanoes erupted with most of the original dinosaurs and A to Z, the prehistoric time had all of the early sages of seeds and venomous predators that were political and take over of States government trillions of years. All day there were take overs just like even worse than the Confederate Army. The original assignment of the Venomous Predators fell off and Al Cappone set it up to go against his enemies. He gained and was recreated trillions of years before he was born in Chicago.

States was set 100%, prehistoric. The computers were designed expensive. The computer of remake went through time trillions and brought in Al Cappone before was States. Al took the biggest enemy of and the location was set to work for him without giving his position or their positions away. The whole package of the Sicilian mafia women and babies were recreated. The system was taken off. Al went to their recreation after death and the star system was recreated. The system was taken and redesigned for the mafia. The mafia was emulated by this government. None of the systems were designed for Al Cappone and later his son, Randy. This location was far into the present at overcoming nature. The prehistoric beasts were different. The life of animals and dinosaurs were A to Z prehistoric before the United States. The president was advanced, the police and the military also. Al Cappone came and went. Randy, during the Confederate Army, bought States prehistoric time in because the mafia was recreated. Before their creation, prehistoric time was A to Z insect, volcano, big snakes and tarantulas, abnormal lizard population, the sand housed predators. The predators were uncanny good with food that was prey. The speciation was from meat to rodents to mice, etc. The military was trained to handle situations. The police fared poorly because their family came in foreign and were released and not charged. They left an opening miles, the military was called in only when the police was killed by the teamsters overtook the police that was educated and seasoned and most with the exception that their family were not broken down and fined and came back that they could do anything they wanted. The Teamsters found gaps and made it through. States utilized a military that was pumped and good within its division. Prehistoric wars was A to Z documented early and predators followed you back to society and decrease you. The crime and war zones were modified in by the United States dramatizing war and presidents being military leaders that cut expected food off and pretended to take them over by being insulting. The United States capability were civilized on foreign. The police were a military against crime in America. The war at the dawn of time kept the future compatible with technology that advanced mankind beyond though.

Time was a factor o Split Second as much as presented there was no real dangers in lifetime outside of the daily grind. Scholastic provided application of output rarely if the assignment wasn't completed. Kids had moods daily work had moods. The computers processed data entry business entry in States. It went beyond time on because States had enemies of brutal force. The processes were advanced beyond time because of strategy. The military was very advanced beyond time and improved prehistoric time and productivity. The strategy of war zones was new and revised every year.

"What happened to Hogan's Heroes?" the President inquired. "Sir that team went to Germany and was deceased immediately. Adolph Hitler's regime was tax evasion America's war fare was young at tactics. The foreign countries were known to be older and wiser at protecting itself. They knew when the United states was founded and the countries output. State collected to the present future, their output was high. The wooded area was fresh. The wildlife was in cages. The insects came in packages contained bait for the zoo populations. Randy Cappone was capable of processing through locations of time trillions a repeat into a future ended. Cindy was in the estates. "Randy" she stated from Hawaii, "remarry if you have to. Bring the government of George Bush in and reprocess it." Randy learned and processed this ability by processing through the Confederate Army money he was legal and a crack at bringing the United States through.

States devised movies, A to Z education in fields processed education output and survival techniques. The actors in the movies were selected by looks, education and were very good public speakers for scholastic. The military processed states growing population. Havana was a location that was lost in time. Havana, like states manifested a zoo of prehistoric that feed off Havana. The civilization was chronic. The music in states was soothing in a dream stage. Randy Cappones dream stage opened to a train that process output and placed you through worlds created through time in Jurassic Park. It was a wonderful night's sleep. The dream state opened seasonally. States cross matched to today's United States. Randy Cappone received permission from all locations to use almost everything he used. A to Z Indiana Jones carried over travel and location through states. Randy married 500 times in three years. The kids were 500 placed in Randy Cappon Estates and paid for their mom's. Cindy was out of freezer units and she and Randy reunited. Randy Cappone added to the United States 100% with the level of F2 and the Sicilian mafia's killing of the Confederate Army. Randy took over the classics, the movies were more compelling and made more sense because States edited in to a society that was smart. The society was complex and future for their today's time. The United States was very modified with repeats. The 2 million races were supposed to turn everything in and went criminal along with the Middle East and were satanic at the end of the regime when the president wanted to process people under ground and make certain their money was legal though the tax department. Time repeated for the tax department o the president since the 1920's had freezer units underground that paused people through time when placed in them. The United States repeated and it was a form of death because they were never recalled. The 2 million populations made it through the underground of the military and cross matched repopulation through the military and cross matched repopulations through the military. Randy froze the United States and processed the repopulations out gaining 100%. Once his money hit the tax department stated you're legal, never give money up to the government. The FBI and military processed people since Randy was 17. It drove him insane because voodoo came from the state department for they went to Satan and repopulation the people in his life that was cross matched. FBI behaves differently and his mind could not file it. As of before and during the confederate army president Bill Clinton processed after signing for warfare with General Grant. The lead general recreated from Hell. The police were underground and repopulated. Randy processed the mafia back in the state police were taken over the city police. The only ones on top of the ground was Randy and his wife Cindy. He and the mafia fought the end of time war and gained through strategies and hours of workmanship, the gun ships of Randy Cappone dropped down in 2 cities, saving the United States from a complete take over. Randy, who processed the movies through and stock. He misunderstood President George Bush's intent. He lived in Monticello, in an apartment at Hillcrest. Apartment 8, he paid 200.00 a month. Cindy Crawford stated "Freeze me through units that paused you until you come back the same age." Before she state that "you can have relationships". J. R. Ewing a fictional character from Dallas and when brought back do not tell her about the relationships or the kids and she would resume with him as her husband. Cindy Crawford was frozen. Cris Perry, Brandon Cappone and Colt. The Sicilian mafia under Al Cappone was frozen for reassignment. They were the same from the 1920's mafia started by Al Cappone. President George Bush was incorporated against the mafia because he was taken seriously at summit meetings. He spoke bad about Randy. Randy spoke bad in public about no one and for no reason, George Bush spoke unkindly. Randy did not support or deny George Bush. He was for America 100% and through programmability he gained against the Confederate Army. The United States was on his side 100%. The take over was Cuba and Middle Eastern countries that wanted to hoard. The Cappone empire and sell organized crime. Randy was one gun, he hired trillions of Sicilian mafia and melted state that went to criminal intent against Randy Cappone. Randy took Shania Twain, country music artist, out of freezer units and incorporated her into capon estates. Randy had permission from his wife Cindy Crawford. Wives never give permission. The reason Cindy did was because they tried t kill him with lethal poisoning and his dad was Al Cappone, the prince of the mafia, known to be dead at age 80. Lexington, KY was a war zone and what lived was nothing what they wanted was Randy to have shock treatment and become poisoned. They wanted to silence him into the government and he was a product of the government since birth. Randy hired on trillions and went through the states department that had no charges and 2 million planets undocumented and foreign Cuba, Colombia, etc. in 2 years. He cross matched the super model agency that sold product into endorsing the product of the Cappone organization, the movies went A to Z up and estates were bought by trillions. Randy married 2 million times and took over millions legally because it was illegal to attack form the Untied States military to Cuba without charges. His defense was high and the money went straight into the government and the tax department. He made money from the movies and was legal from the start and had no charges.

Al hired teams to bring money back to him when the state department tried stealing it. The mafia was educated cons and very masculine and could handle themselves in aggressive locations. Their output with the crime syndicate was high. The Smith and Wesson gun play made their output 100%. The biggest army ever to syndicate. Chicago crime went up with Al Cappone's crime syndicate. The reason they were successful was, they hit 100% against the enemy and let their families live, henceforth, most other organizations was illegal, killed off people that was for them in life, henceforth contradicting themselves. The organized crime killed off on moods and claiming their titles in a civilized society. Knowing your job assignment was easily determined and finances that paid for your output of cars for making it to work, bill paid electricity, water company and clothes. Gangs claimed by drug sell illegal. If you found out why it was illegal and substituted it for legal, you did not have to worry about incarceration. The State Department, an educated department, set out to weed out substance that's bad for you and declared it was not conductive to your health. It was as drugs brought in to the United States by foreigners from a country it was produced in and it caused addiction. Scholastic had an 8 hour melt down on education that output a channel for workmanship and output in a legal America that promoted to your life. There was stress and output on the job in being synced in a family from the oldest to the youngest. The social occasions brought tension sometimes it bite in the middle of the night and ate at consciousness. A to Z America, form New York to Los Angeles to Florida, provided a country that developed through the state department hospitalization and state department services, tension in traffic, tensions in dating equal to skills we gained with authority and discipline. If it improved our output usually it improved a company with workmanship. Organized discipline gave output that improved if your personal life was kept up with. It gave consistency so we didn't stay awake form lack of discipline we showed up on time and was accounted for. Personal choices were good if kept restocked and paid for and improved, training became mechanical or automatic if trained in that area, you had scope and defined the job quality. It was expected to be an executive you was considered normal and personified in that area of jobs, of skills and finances. The TV and movies even books were great to become a character and not take life seriously. For the amount of time fiction overtook you and you were allowed to dream music could tantalize the mind and memory, however chosen. Superstition was powerful in some location of the United States. People usually knew the tangibles of their physical universe and fact and fiction of output. Randy was capable of traveling through the United States through the world over to the present day. States help character, past, present and future and hid through time. The United States was told to turn in other locations to Jehovah and went to Satan and was frozen after the take over another world was created. The Confederate army made it thorough Eastern countries. The movies improved through Randy. He rewrote them and the actors went into a future studio and narrated 100% like a radio show host. They gained millions and the movies were authentic. The fist digitally mastered was Tony Montana in Scarface. That netted a lot of money because it was an original and made 500 million dollars. Al Pacino was paid a lot of money and turned it back in and was okayed paid. Randy took the character with an IBM system and played Tony Montana. With Florida estates, he bought 925 houses when Al Pacino's Scarface became popular as a re-introduction. Cindy Crawford was met at the Hyatt Regency in Lexington and lived in the Hawaiian estates. Tony Montana's story was beyond time in Florida. The military processed Tony into the country from Cuba to place the other drug dealers from America out of business. He was given his agenda of weaponry to kill opposition. His family was a Cuban family, a mother, a sister that was pretty. Scarface, Al Pacino was the same. He was mafia and against the state was what the mafia meant. He was Cuban and usually the Cubans were gracious and courteous because they knew the language. He learned the language well and was equipped venomous. He dressed well and presented cocksure. After the George Bush administration upon going or moving form apartment 203 to Hillcrest, President Obama bequeathed him military, FBI, the head of the police and legal mafia. He was Al Cappone's son. Tony Montana was recreated or frozen though time to age 80. His time came trillion of years ago. Scarface was the same, yet it did not mention that he had 10 brothers that looked like him. Randy brought them in and asked if they would work for him. They said they would. Tony stated no stipulations. Randy said I will pay you. Tony and his 10 brothers that looked like him was crack at take over the state department and handing it back to the Italian mafia and Randy Cappone and Al Cappone organizations of the mafia. George Bush was mostly kidding when he spoke of war games, yet a location that was proven one of 9 planets system presented themselves and were not documented as only a planet with a ring around it, unknown to be civilized. If a location like this presented itself, uncalled for and unexplained, you could cross match overtakes in organizations like the FBI, an organization of state meant they overtook to extract something through the president. The FBI was crime, Roman Catholic was stage with the Christians. The Roman Catholics staged profits of high accord that stated God was very powerful. In districts of foreign religions was failed because the locations of Saturn, the nine planets on world one they choose God none. The United States was supposed to end those locations, chose Satan as did the Middle East. The people went to units to freeze through time and did so and came out year after year, an army of Satan's United States repeated. The Confederated army, the south from Hell ended time eternity wanted to recreate and other location of planets went Satan's way. One million one hundred worlds of the United States. These locations came out of freezer units to overcome in Satan's name. Randy, Al, Mark Lawlor and Jimmy Grider won over the Confederate army. Randy lived in Monticello and left Mark and Jimmy in offices. Satan's men came in and one of the surprised Mark and busted him in the nose. He was surprised. Jimmy saw it from his office and stated "I thought that you could fight!" Randy was asleep. He wore a Smith and Wesson.44 sub machine gun. Al stated freeze the mafia for reassignment in the location of Middle East.

During the latter part of the Bush Administration, Randy missed Cindy 100%. They connected a perfect combination from Lexington. Cindy went back to Los Angeles after Lexington. The township of Lexington wanted Randy dead. He was frowned upon as Sicilian mafia from the Hope center to homeless shelters that he live in for one year. Upon leaving Lexington there was zero alive. The city repopulated in two weeks and automatically again form graves filling up its probably automatically today. Looking over the record they remodeled and repopulated the city.

At apartment 8 in Monticello, Randy was speaking to Cindy in Hawaii. He noticed black magic, a devil, was constructing a building. He mentioned to Cindy and she suggested telling Al Cappone, he stated that he would handle it. The two got through on the president s military live 100% form Hawaii to Monticello. She took care of Randy's son, Colt. States provided shelter when a country Randy defended came in on him. The location of FBI, the military and the Middle East began war for against Randy Cappone for no reason.

There was no charges. He was a loose cannon for the mob and succeeded by guts and determination.

The Bush administration was told that the Sicilian mafia was involved in no warfare games. Randy was for the Untied States 100% and had no charges. The president wanted everything of the Sicilian mafia dead; Randy, Cindy, Cris, Brandon, and Colt. His family was frozen, George Bush thought that Al Cappone was the head gun and leader of the mafia and that he could take him over easily. Randy ran the mafia and was crack at it. George Gush thought that he could maintain respect that was lost with Randy, Al Cappone, Mark Lawler and Jimmy Grider fighting the Confederate army war. The Gulf War was edited through time. George Bush in Monticello was 38 pounds over-weight. Randy ate lowfat 5 days a week and had a high output. The United States in history had a high output in warfare and came in 100% on Randy. He picked up all titles of government from the military. The reason he could not get back to states was Brittany Spears, a girlfriend while Cindy was out of commission, accidentally turned off the transport to the future. The button was pushed, the side took Randy to the worst location of criminals ever. The side was like a car that rolled down the first organization was the Hell's Angels. The Hell's Angels were the very worst criminals ever to die in Satan's name. The Angels were great with weapons and very skilled at crime. The devil too theme park music and went beyond crime. You can check out any time you like but you can never leave. Randy hid in a dumpster for hours and watched their style. Brittany woke up to aerobics, high in a mountainous terrain. Beyond time, this location was outdated and fresh. The housing was expensive. The scholastic of the future, a teacher spoke of Randy, where meeting was through the future of F2, a level of safety for the hostages against the Confederate Army.

Randy guarded the United States against criminal law and an overtake of time. Randy was a prisoner of the past if he died while in a past United States, he would never see Cindy Crawford or their son Colt again. The Sicilian mafia would be frozen in time forever. He began to wonder if he would live to see snow in Indiana or Christmas again. Randy let zero fear fill his every sense. He was out of his league. The theme music of Hotel California was haunting his life. Since and after Lexington and the FBI trying to arrest him because his dad was Al Cappone was all a distant memory. The Confederate Army overtake and a seven year war that kept time going. Upon moving to Monticello, George Bush, a politician for the war fare edited in by him and fought by the Sicilian mafia, vanished deep into a sea long ago with no hospitalization and no support. In Monticello, he saw George Bush meddling in Congress and was caught by Randy 100%. Randy was legal, his money was obtained by movies. George Bush's army from Hell that was hostile in Monticello without charges was shot. When he tried to intimidate Randy and the first casualty of war was replaced by a mechanical and 500 marines when an act of war played in Monticello. Al Cappone was frozen and the mafia, Cindy, Cris, and the kids were frozen. Bill States did not see the Smith and Wesson.44 when the sub-machine gun barked, Randy was like a rattlesnake. The body fell and was replaced automatically. The FBI replaced Cindy. The double could not get into the trillion dollar estate. The visions came of Cindy being hostage as Fidel Castro took over the United States. The mafia gun ships were future and dissolved Fidel in hours. The gun ships glided through time and dropped. The bodies were picked up and the United States was automatic. Colombia came and 2 million of the most future locations never proven to exist. The mind dissolved when the enemies black magic and were ate into the core. Trillions of Italians that were young were hired by Randy. The guns increased racketeering to 100% and the whole United State was taken by Randy.

The Joker came a long time ago with one hundred zeros was one of the highest numbers ever computed. The Joker's reign was trillions in Gotham's present day. The Joker showed up in Marvel Comics and on other locations of time. He played anything that dominated and lived one trillion years longer than Satan and was meaner and a bigger criminal. His venom was a dominant black widow tarantula, more powerful than Satan. Randy recreated him and he worked for him as his right hand man. Humans were weak for the tarantula and the enemy was who the Joker was, he was for Randy. His diet was one feeder cow a day. The nutrient the spider that became the enemy craved was the blood of humans, of the Sicilian mafia's blood. He was criminal in the most evil way, an insect with strength 1000x compared to humans. He thought of humans the same we would think of chocolate cake. The Joker knew who the enemy was and became them.

The mafia was the biggest military assigned to Chicago and location to the United States, the Confederate army was past tense 100 trillion times built from a rural South, trained to overcome a country that repeated and was ended by Satanism. When the Southerners felt their churches failed and the military of the United States one trillion came inot their houses and shot them and after embalmed, Satan recreated them in his image to overtake God, who failed for them and kill time in a country that ended the South. The mafia that was active, was Al Cappone, Mark Lawlar, and Steve Grider. Randy was their leader. The gun ships had billions of trained military men that defended the Cappone empire. The three assigned were crack. The United States was hostage for 7 years. The generals were complex and killers that killed quick. The Hatfields and McCoys were trillions and took on whole States. Jed Calmpett was a comedy on TV. He had a gun and a confederate army that killed States of the United States in minutes. The South gained in the past 100% of the time they were devils. Montana, the anchorman for The Running man, had an audience from the Theme Park the Hotel California.

Randy Cappone is a stowaway from the future. He came back to our present time to hide form a politician that wanted him to report in. The previous night Tony Montana shackled Randy to a cell and smashed his face. The Cuban mafia was devils. Randy sank into a dark pit and was beaten. Sodium pentothal was shot into his arm. They extracted information 100%. Tony continued the studio was a game show the lights were color, the audience was angry; they wanted Randy dead.

"Mr. Montana", the pretty supermodel Patty whispered in his ear. "Yes?" he replied. One large muscled man in the crowd shouted, "Tony's going to get some love" Tony held his hand up. "This is not a sporting event. This guy came to avoid a government over organizations of State that he was the boss of. He did not follow his commander-in-chief, the President. Randy was surprised that Montana knew anything about him. He had a black eye and forgot the sodium pentothal. He joked with people that he was David Cassidy's brother. He was beaten by the Cuban mafia. "Randy Cappone was a take over complete. We caught the weasel before he got out of the chicken house in our present time with information systems and technology" The supermodel, Patty Anderson begged for Randy. The Sodium pentothal revealed that Randy thought of Richard Gere in such a way the audience roared and applauded. Randy's ears burnt as the information was revealed. Tony spoke to the muscular marine in the audience, "Do you want to say something to Randy?" "Yes, the President wants to speak to you." Randy tried to smile but was too sore. "OK" he stated, "What's your favorite movie?" the marine asked. "Freejack, the opposition should have won." "Freejack!" the marine responded. "The villain should have won." The marine frowned, "I caught that. An educated society and had free jack" the crowd cheered. It bit into Randy's nervous system. "Do you want to be in a movie?" the marine asked. Randy stated "Yes." "Well sign up"

"What is it Patty? What were you going to say a few minutes ago?" Tony asked. Patty smiled. She was pretty, her makeup flawless. "Stephen King, the announcer of Horror Masterpiece Theater, wants to talk to you". "What is it?" Tony asked. "Would you like to be in a movie?" Stephen King asked. "Yes" Tony Montana asked "OK well do it." He looked at Randy. "Try to maintain yourself, Mr. Big Villian, don' pee yourself. I hope you die". The crowd laughed and agreed to Randy's death. The FBI was in the darkness with weapons. The leader was Steve Garret. He drew plans out. The Hell's Angels would contend with him and the Confederate army that came in trillions and were good with weaponry and death. Tony Montana met with Stephen King who announced The Horror Theater at Halloween. The agency gave him the contracts and the Running Man announced their organization was signed for a movie. "You should be on for a movie that goes into drug deals". Tony sighed. That meant that they could go into his life and memories and use him in the movies. Randy Cappone, Al Cappone's only son was caught. His chance of winning was zero. Brittany Spears was not set to return to his apartment in Monticello and would live and die in States. The reason he remarried was because he was convinced that Cindy was in favor of it and was frozen.

Randy was abducted in his sleep. He ran illegal with a criminal law record. He was issued immunity. His boss centralized crime. The country was abducted for tow weeks to witness a government taken over by the organized crime Sicilian mafia. Our countries chances of an output and factors of a foreign take over would regress and the future of our present would become brighter. It was believe that Randy kept people well with family units designed by him on F2. His illegal was killing the enemies without incarceration or a trial.

The lights were a future to disco. The area had strobe lights and brilliant lights affiliated with drugs, medication was a self help treatment of clearing your mind. It processed Satan and channel to the devil was how it was used. Concert had light shows that were dazzling and promoted to music. The Running Man operated trillions all day in finances. The idea was to bleed Randy of the future and give themselves eternity and for present time in the United States not to happen. The strategies were drawn out by the State department from this United States President to the state police and the military. The sodium pentothal worked and they knew precisely who he was and they knew his output because they went through F2 for 3 weeks and knew that Al Cappone assisted in running franchises. Randy lived in Albany, Kentucky and worked as a waiter and dish washer before and after the movies to make money and to stay active. He was very nice to them. They were brought through for assistance. He fed them, clothed them and sent back well.

Brittany was slim built. Her navel was sensual. She wore swim wear almost and looked triple A good looking. She bit her lip and wondered what happened to Randy. States came in through the iced ocean cool the trees were refreshment in ovadazation. She was in estates that cost trillions all of the women of Randy Cappone were set to be with other guys. In his life time, he meant to establish with only Cindy. When the government came in on his and Mr. Bush tried strategies to humiliate in front of the Senate, etc., he shut him down the last thing. Cindy stated before being frozen was remarry just don't go against me. Randy thought about Cindy. The estates were 925 houses. The food processors grew food and coffee from rich soils around the planet and harvested quick and by computer were processed into plates and garnished AAA, a genesis alpha program grew crops overnight and they came out apple orchard golden and never ran out. From Randy cell almost unconscious, he thought of scholastics Christmas Santa's in a frosty window, summers in Indiana, soybeans and corn sectioned off, bee hives loaded with sweet honey. The yellow buses on cold frosty mornings, scholastic going on throughout the day. Randy was half between conscious and sleep. He thought that he would die. He remembered the aroma of Thanksgiving pies, even though he tried to modify sweets out of his diet. The mall of the Hotel California filled up the adult entertainment was used to capacity.

The paper ran stories on Randy and his programs. One percent of the country was against him. Randy barely escaped the Hell's Angels who was he stole a bike upon their attention being turned and rode it at 25 miles an hour. He didn't know if he missed a gear or did not know how to ride in the future. Randy parked the bike in an alley and took a subway deep into Los Angeles. He through that he was as hours away he was apprehended easily he felt that he stood out like a sore thumb. The truth was, he was viewed by cameras everywhere and the Hell's Angels followed his progress and found him. Tony Montana laughed, "It was like finding a baby!" he sneered. Tony and the military placed him in a cage. The city of Los Angeles saw him by a video phone system and applauded. "He's a big criminal!" The Hell's Angeles laughed. The City of Los Angeles lit up and fell to darkness. Randy had a cell full of hay. He tried burning himself. Tony wore a very impressive suit and smelled of rich colognes. He wore the attire for the Host of the Running Man and could kill Randy at any time. He looked at him form dark Cuban eyes. "I can see you, you are a gamer, your organized crime did not assist you here to steal workmanship. What we want and are going to get is nothing but incarcerated down. Organized crime, you couldn't back it, The Running Man starts early tomorrow. Get some rest." The Cuban walked away. He was clean and muscular. A Cuban army with weapons and sold and spent high for a criminal. Tony's brothers were ten and supported him. Randy's state faded. He tried to meditate and go deep into his conscious and experience high. The Cuban stated sternly, "Are you practicing Zen Buddhism or a foreign mediation, or is it a self help that releases you and places us in our grave?" A big military went through his mind. He woke up and looked around. A cat fell down and crunched leaves. It looked weird and scurried away. Fever set in. Randy's resistance was down and his system was invaded by a flu virus. Rain fell. The enemy was cool. Randy shivered. Tony was speaking to his brother "How's Cappone?" he asked. "He's breaking down. His systems were very expensive. He was modified the finest of the future U. S. A. year I believe 2000 and something. He was valued that he brought the Untied States through hundred of times. He achieved high and overachieved. He was a crack at overtakes of the country. His systems were beyond the horizon. We all have to die sometime. He's trapped. The future's best agent, like a fish in a net. We have him, he's a baby." The Montanas were 10 communists that out sold American dealers and placed them out of business. Their warfare was high. They were like spiders that trapped their victims. Their weaponry skills were high.

The Joker came and went trillions of years. He was bred a killer. He webbed and killed Gotham in seconds. He was a black spider with an orange spot on his back that dominated in all areas and consumed humans. He dropped socially in second and remade others. There was no religion. He was the ultimate authority of each era. The movies he was in was Korshak, the Night Stalker. He succeeded in crime 100% of the time and was the biggest criminal of all time. He was in Batman and dominated Gotham. He was the biggest evil ever and outlived Satan before Satan's creation by trillions of years and was terrible, more evil. Batman, Spiderman and Superman were given to him to weed out crime. He would have in seconds and went back to his web and ate cows. Society turned on him and tried to exterminate him. He knocked political science out by the millions in seconds and dominated for trillions of years. Randy looked his record up. He was dead when the oxygen ran out in Gotham. Randy recreated him and he worked for him as a right hand man. He was good. Randy's system went to the government that was the U. S. A. trillions. The estates of Cappone housed 500 kids by supermodels that were AAA 3 a day, impregnated and paid for set for the enemy before being frozen, Cindy stated "you can remarry and get even J. R. Ewing style" and Randy did. Some of the women were popular and high in their fields such as Shania Twain, Jennifer from the Dukes of Hazard, Southern women that were prominent, well blossomed and princesses for the drug field of marijuana. He progressed miles in the Sicilian mafia and made money legal from the movies. His output was 100%. Time was effective and affected by him 100%. Morning came in a future that came and went beyond sun up sundown. The picnics with family and friends with baskets full of cold cuts, coolers with ice and foods. Grills full of hamburgers, steaks and hot dogs. The estates in Hawaii had cinamoes, food processors work out A to Z. Cindy called Randy in Albany, KY. The Confederate army was in Alabama. They would soon attack 25 states. Memories were in Randy's mind. His wound healed some, the flu cleared some. Tony opened his cell door. "Come on, come on, come on!" Tony stated he wore a fresh suit. His persona was high. They went into his office.

"This is Stephen King". King smiled. "Sign her for the Running Man." Randy signed. "It's for Stephen King's Horror Theater. We'll pick up real life." He shook his hand. The rooms filled with detectives, police and military. All exits were blocked. He paid attention to no pretty woman. He knew that they were taken. None were built as well as Cindy Crawford, his wife. She was frozen and stayed young to 23 at 43. Brittany was very attractive in States growing up. He appreciated the vows of matrimony, yet through the mafia and success in the movies, things were differently organized. Randy and Cindy were very smart and very grounded and Randy never really used anyone. He was as captive as being in jail present day and escape was very scarce of happening. They broke all systems by a computer programmer. He was lost far into the past.

"The Running Man", stated Tony Montana. Randy Cappone could barely stand, he was too weak and beaten up. The FBI was after him because of Lexington, the Confederate Army because he was against the biggest military from Hell trying to overtake time. The administration and the State department was big. The police had weapons trained on him.

Re-enter Brittany was very cute. Her ruin was kissing Madonna. She said it was edited in. Randy was at his and Brittany Spears housing in states. "What happened?" she asked. Time returned to normal in the United States one trillion with no memory of Randy. He could barley stand. Brittany held him, he thanked her and he headed t the shower to clean up.

The Running Man repeated one million, one hundred times. It's purpose was to get criminal law to 0 and play a criminal that usually got by with crime. They played them out of any dignity they could to where usually they won. They were confronted and lost. An example would be to play Charles Manson out of his brutal murders and publicly was his loss, and defeat and taking crime away. Henceforth the Hotel California had units t melt away crime y being confronted by trained state department officials. Randy healed up in weeks. He went back to the Untied States. Brittany had his kids. Shania Twain, Jessica from the Dukes of Hazard, the supermodel agency released the top super models. Sarah Evans had his kids. Martina McBride, Demi Moore A to Z triple A woman had his kid. He paid for the kids 100% and was very respectful and was very humble when he moved to an apartment in Hillcrest, apt. 8, Monticello. He planned to spend time with Cindy and his kid Colt. The president came in. Cindy was frozen as was Colt, Cris Perry and Branndon and his family was frozen for protective reasons. The FBI tried to play his family and died. Saturn came in and tested the United States. Their technology was high. The United States was unsuspected and had flab. The Saturn population was taking over. They took over when the president took people underground in cubicles and starved them of food and the president processed money from the tax department. Saturn and 2 million locations in space that turned in nothing when the Confederate Army took over and killed during world one of the Unite States. Also foreigners went Satan's way and was frozen through time. The United States was afraid one night and asked for help. Randy froze them at 2:30 am and was groggy. He forgot and when he woke up Fidel Castro repopulated. He looked like President Bush and the United States. The Untied States came back 1 year and a half later. George Bush came back and Obama was president.

Randy copied the United States one thousand times. He went in at locations through states technology that no one could. He smarted from the Hotel California. He was caught futurizing by a state department that wanted to feed crime back through a state cop and reduce his whole life to nothing because he was caught in a future location with a country that was reorganized. Brittany bought his reasoning back. He tried working out more, keeping his stamina up and recruiting ideas that incorporated the mafia in ways that defended the Estates of Cappone. The reason the mafia's output was legal in the state was because their enemies were real and they were 100% out to kill them. Their output was effective against the enemy. The mafia was organized crime, syndicated the United States 100%. They were shadows of death against any enemy that went against them. The song, Hotel California played through time trillions of years after. The movies, record contracts, the adult theme park, Randy smarted good from his capture. Brittany saved his life. He appreciated that lots. Cindy Crawford was taken out of freezer units. She stated before when Randy moved to Monticello, to freeze her and to set the programs to equal relationship for the enemy that went against the family. She stated "Set everything J. R. Ewing style to get even with the enemy, you can remarry, just don't go against me" He knew he would tear the government down, the reason was George Bush was meeting with the Senate and he was very disrespectful to Randy Cappone. His dad, Al Cappone, was frozen and one billion mafia. George Bush was very degrading and Randy was for the Untied States and legal. George met over 500 times and Randy caught every one and caught the United States coming in on him at apartment 8 in Monticello. Barrack Obama was president and Cindy was brought back. His son, Colt, Cris Perry and their son Branndon. Randy was at the fairgrounds at Albany, KY, at an apartment. Cindy was in Hawaii. He introduced her to treatment that ran in the estates to process better, her money was high from super modeling. His first movie was Tony Montana, a remake of Scarface. Tony's wife was Italian, Cuban and Randy played his son, Emmanuel, Italian Cuban. Tony was 65. Al Pacino was paid editing. Cindy played Sydney, an attorney that got the mafia off on technicality. Cris Perry played Emmanel's wife. Another movie depicted Lexington, the state department tried lethal poison for Randy in a glass as well as Cindy Crawford. Randy had Smith and Wesson sub-machine gun derringers that hid. He killed them 100% in the Eastern State poison zone. The Federal Bureau of Investigation, under President Bill Clinton tried lethal poison. The only one left alive was Cindy Crawford. A new shift came into Eastern State. The bodies were disposed of by the mafia. Alive out of Lexington when Randy left a halfway house in Lexington to make a 3 hour drive with his aunt was zero was alive. The FBI deceased 100%. They had no charges. Cindy went back to Los Angles. She and Randy were married. They saw each other rarely. He met Cris Perry at a restaurant in Albany, KY. She had his first kid Branndon. President Clinton signed for warfare with the Confederate Army that could not be proven to exist that ended time with the Middle East and 2 million star systems. The country was replaced by a cross match of the confederate army, the devils became the United States while the Untied States stayed underground. The war was won by Randy Cappone in 7 years. He processed George Bush in Monticello and George Bush upon the end of his term came out of freezer units with the United States Barrack Obama stated that Randy kept is titles.

Mark Bowlin

President Mark Bowlin met well with the staff and the vice president Richard Adams, about the economy. He spoke to the military about the Middle East. His suit fit well. The United States was known to be the richest country in the world, warfare was expert, the state department worked well for the president, a well oiled team brought the United States in economy and workmanship to number one in most areas. "Hi Sir. You have a council meeting in five minutes" The President's limousine arrived; he kept his security light, with a high output for protection. "Welcome to the President," he shook the President's hand. "My name is Richard Baker." The president smiled and nodded. "Thank you very much, Richard. O.K., let's begin. Your thoughts, your actions, your nervous system, your output, we as council would like for you to process well and leave thinking well. Medicine is non addictive if you take it when you leave. The important part is, at work, you stay awake, at night you sleep. Anti-depressants are non addictive. Alcoholics can take them and stay sober. As a state organization, we suggest violence toward your family none, or that you do nothing illegal. We hope that you learn to process better in your life and feel better and when you leave, process better at home. You gain in society if you know that if on a academic level if you went through time at any time, you would find out that we as humans are not that imposed to dramatics. We succeed with appropriate education in a job we are trained in for 3 weeks. We are not dramatic. School systems provide education and the locations are bland. The education you receive does not allow mental illness, until you're sixteen or seventeen and can not process your data well. You get up suit up and go to school. Dramatics are for the movies. Manic depression and mental illness is the field of doctors. Manic becomes bipolar. If it's high highs and low lows, what if example you found out that it was caffeine and your habits of consumption caused you to stay awake at night? It's only a theory yet if we watch our habits. Mental illness is treatable with medicine." The next meeting of the president was the military of the United States. We became powerful in war because the United pulled together from the military and the announcement of the war and when the war was over, the United States pulled together and we as a country won. The military strategies were complex. From the commander-in-chief to the highest general to the private, the country worked well like clock work. The military of the United States was A1. The state department including schools and police were in order. This made the president very happy. The Vice-president, the President and his staff meet in the boardroom. The president spoke from behind the podium. "Turn that mike on! I can't hear you" Senator Bob Augustine from Birmingham, Alabama stated. 'Thank you very much" "Where are you from originally?" "Wisconsin" "Why can't Birmingham elect senators from that location?" the President Mark Bowlin asked. "Because they wanted to be represented by someone that did not speak Southern, that could get Birmingham through. The President turned on the mike. The room filled up. "Welcome delegates. Any issues?" The Vice President rose. "Permission to address the President on current issues." "Do so Vice-President Erwin," the President stated. The room grew silent. The delegates, senators, governors and state department were presented masculine and feminine and their wives and husbands. They dressed very nice in suits and clothing that was expensive. Their salaries were expensive. The food and restaurants usually appointments and reservations were secretarial in job output. The politicians were stylish, polished and professional. The Vice President spoke, "With our staff meeting out of the way" The President waved "go on". "Thanks to the President. The Middle East supplies the demands for oil and the wars are under control," the Vice president spoke of issues thoroughly for 2 hours, bathroom breaks provided along with cafeteria eating that was trays sent by Washington's finest restaurants. The food was slid on a cart cafeteria-style and handed out like a hospital handed out food. The Vice President spoke of safety issues, hospitalization, every thing form seat belt to space travel to the moon. NASA had not been on the news since the 70's and the presidency of Richard Nixon, who was president after the Vietnam War and was impeached after long meetings with Watergate. The Vice President was through and covered issues well. Reports were issued clean and neat to the state department with the president's government approved signature. The folders handed out on Washington's report were to upgrade the on state issues presented by the President and his staff. "We went to the moon and developed shuttles. There are no wars going on and we have no real changes if we could reactivate the moon program or should I say space program, we could reincorporate the United States through technology of space travel to other planets" the President suggested.

"That's a pipe dream Sir. First of all we do not have an education in space travel. NASA and factories that produce moon and space travel takes years and affiliation with the nine planets are distant and we do not know if they exist. NASA and the astronauts would be concerned of oxygen or the food supply running out. The need of a doctor would be a concern. There's also the probability of getting out there and nothing existing and not making it back." the Vice president voice his concerns.

The President began, "We have three years in this term. I want my presidency to be known to have achieved something." "What if it fails?" the Vice president asked. The president studied the Vice president and stated, "If it fails, we can play Neil Armstrong and space exploration. Our successes or our failure and ask the new to move on and the press report from the military." The military spokesperson Don Richardson was very serious about military affairs. The major spoke "The Middle East is happy with product sales, the President association on trade paid off." "Thank you. It's good to be complimented. Please continue. "Thank you, Mr. President. The Middle East receiving trade has no charges. The floods are minimized, we are in excellent shape o the military output and America is running well." "Bravo!" the President stated, "That's precisely what I want"

The space program of NASA was deep in the Artic, at an island that was modified. NASA headquarters for testing. The space travel went deep into the island and processed in like a submarine went deep into the sea. At NASA headquarters, the command was looking into a computer that showed the team in the Artic on the video screen that brought in the space exploration, millions of miles into the ocean on an island uninhabited. The team was one thousand. The space travel indicated by a factory computer millions of units for space travel. The navy helped set this first unit up and the engineers processed the plans through and the factory came out with full units. NASA loaded in orders to process the units out and the distance entered to make it to one of the 9 planets. The president spoke to the military went to meetings and endorsed the Untied States 100%. The press meetings, he spoke well of the United States to foreigners. He wore a black suit, a black tie and a white shirt. He had glasses on and appeared the nerdy virty. He designed his house after anything prehistoric time. It went down to sub basement and had al varieties of estates of billions. The cars and gates and service workers was what he called them. He called them that and asked them to come Monday and Friday on lawn care and housekeeping. His money came form computer company was Diamond Computer stated to be a gem. A diamond symbol on the computer stated it was an original. His name was Stephen Louis. He barely made it second generation money by mistake his output in school and education was good. He picked up a volume of computer store by mistake. The reason was he processed Dungeons and Dragons through and picked up a computer store He thought that he would drop it and go back to live with his parents after completing the video program. A friend of his, Ricky Adams and other helped He knew them from school and assumed that they were assigned to him by classroom projects at college. The employees stayed from the previous company and drew out plans. He named the company Diamonds. The video was beautiful artwork of wondrous castles with waterfalls and brilliance called Dungeons and Dragons. The pinball sold high at arcades. The video game sold well. Ricky Adams organization was Dungeons and Dragons and he knew the criteria. His house was bought and emulated prehistoric time. Dungeons and Dragons was a registered trademark of Stephens. He had the criteria of the organization and ran it how he wanted. Stephen held meetings in his boardroom, his finances were high and he had them set to never run out and the money to make it through time. He looked over the roomful of people. "Hi, our organization of Dungeons and Dragons meant basement and blast. You must speak t the dungeon master, me to proceed in computers. You are the team that backs me". The crowd applauded. "We buy, absorb and present the best of the future to this present day. You are my team and I expect we will be the biggest in computer espionage and take overs. Our programmers at Diamond are expert. We have the facility to back the organization in all capacities. We can write computers through movies and video basketball teams, the military and the police. We make teams from the movies that Diamond will put out. It is a lot of work. You will be on the clock. Full shifts, the supervisors will be tough and you will be replaced if you output is not adequate. We pay at Diamond." Stephen Louis had his estate done well. The ten floors had one floor that snowed up, none that could be burnt, flooded or the military could not get in. He kept it in emergency. It was foolproof and set to last one hundred years, nobody could get in. Illegal organizations that were popular were the police departments to apprehend and knew the whereabouts to file out and in according to what was done and prosecuted.. If organizations were around since the 70's, you could wonder their true roots and how they made it through time.

The state department administration would have loved to have the state department on directory A to Z, it was impossible to do, they were on salary or worked full shifts and did not want to be synched into a directory or a government level. Rickey Adams had them on computer, their job titles, job experience, their state families, location and phone number. The state issued everything needed for the state schools, police departments and the military. The state paid for by the state was equipment. The employees were paid by the state. The state progressed with a big army of state department's employees. The president ran the country well and the state processed a legal United States to the best of the state departments ability and education. Tax evasion was the ultimate zero for some Americans. They were at one time out going and liked kids became a dislike for kids and wanted them out of their lives. The truth of tax evasion was the person had a money problem only. Remaining legal and out of the penitentiary, they could re-earn during their next pay.

Stephen Louis knew as an educated man, the duration of naming his organization a Satanist organization. The police department classified that he was legal and paid for the companies overtaken. His agenda was known, his parties and banquets were paid for with legal money. His offices and employees were paid for with legal money. His house was paid for. It was brilliant in sublevels. His cars went with it expensive so what, they got him to work and parties. You called them junk if they apparently did not run well. If Ricky caught a ride with someone and the drier was apologetic for not being on the radio. Ricky stated "It does not bother me" and it did not. The point was that a car took you from your house to your office or restaurant or engagement. If you hired someone to drive the limousine was a popular car service for escort and maintenance. The important part was if business was conducted 98 percent of the time, you parked in a parking garage and your car went unseen if you dressed accordingly to business, you got business through according to your boss's agenda of uniformed style of dress. Cars were transport that got you there and back. The food quietly and output of the company was credited to the president.

NASA sand deep below artic freeze in America. The system was picked up by medium computers the government bought at the computer store. NASA programmed it through time. The advancement was beyond time for present year. The ice was thick, the ocean cold and deep into the soil. NASA tested their space travel and gain interest that were conducted.

The FBI was very good at processing crime out of the government, absorbing games and breaking them down. The court dates were set, the government received permission from Epic movies to style themselves from actors in the movies, and infiltrate crime. The capabilities to look stylish like the crime organization that was absorbed. After assignment, they could go home and look like themselves and pay bills for an 8 hour a day job and know that they processed crime out and helped the Untied States well The organization was educated in crime. They checked with local police forces if they could with leaks to the crime in which the crime organization could hide crime. The crime prevention organization was very educated and did a community. The FBI had offices in every state, their morals were high. They had government funding, a government seal from the president and an output that was a police force that could knock an army out and process it through the United States court system, summons and court date. They were legal and educated at spotting crime and coercing it out. The FBI had offices in all states and some Middle Eastern countries. The military backed them if foreign affairs, they were the president's finest. The FBI was not after discrimination when married they cheated on their wives none. They procreated only if the criminal's wife was not illegal. The procreation was off they fantasized with the woman none if charged and the report in they seldom went back on a case. The agent of the

FBI would do police work as a police detective, that just gathered information for the police. The FBI also wore uniforms legally. The task force was improved and was valued by the police as an outlet against crime. The United States Marines had a high output, the navy was mated with wives, most of the military was mated with women and had a high output. They were absolutely against the enemy and gained on 3 shifts of 8 hours changing 3 times a day. Their jobs were precise, their education geared for their job. The Air Force dropped down perfectly on navigation and the military worked like clockwork. The islands of the oceans were test grounds for NASA Space Program. The vessels were constructed like a bomb shelter by the navy in the sea. The NASA program constructed subs that could contain the sea, the saltwater oxygen for flooding that had vehicles and everything NASA needed for 9 planetary systems. The systems were assembled by a military factory. The engineers designed them with the presidents orders once one was assembled completely and tested. The factory had the design and could assemble 100 units a day. The NASA Space Travel Units were placed in a computer with the units full. The commander could by computer, send the units anywhere he wanted. The head of NASA was Col. Tim James. He organized NASA space travel with a team that could take it to the ocean and bring back the samples and proof of their existence. James was a no nonsense man that knew how to place a team together for high results. He was interested in personality, very little, job results, very highly. He played by the book and stayed legal in the state department ad designed teams that did the same. His reports to the president were accurate and he worked a full 8 hour shift. He utilized results highly. The reason he did not deviate from laws was because there was plenty of leeway on being legal in the country. The teams were big. The previous night, he took the computer that looked like a radar to keep enemy planes out of the country and dropped one of NASA below the hemisphere of Mars. It went undetected and he would leave it sunk into Mars with an automatic crew. To place NASA leagues ahead of the time schedule.

Tim contacted the president and gave him a repot and kept Washington informed. The NASA team had to fend an open receiver on other star systems or planets to receive the signal and the system picked up NASA system and the radar sent produced the orders and the computer searched for and found the necessary components for drop NASA Space Program. If the radar sensor could not find the adequate details and parts, the computer generated radar returned not received. The NASA system was very good at detail and undetectable. NASA made it for the first time to another planet.

The president was happy. He could ask the news eventually to edit the first moon exploration and hopefully the samples of the other planets. The police department stayed in contact internationally from the United States and the state department. Word from Mars is the location exists with civilization. The military was high in output. The FBI was high at crime prevention. The teams worked well together, well oiled with high output. NASA space travel made it to Mars. "Welcome to International World News!" the anchorman's name was Dan Miller. "Good evening, NASA was capable by a radar system that sank NASA space station into the artic, to send NASA and touch down on Mars. They accredited our space travel and the president is happy"

Lou Bales

"Thanks Dan. We have footage from NASA's exploration. NASA went far into the distance with radar space travel." A man came on that looked very relived. He had his hands clasped behind his head. "Our team is at a location on Mars that is high in oxygen and very civilized. Our travel unit is called NASA's finest. We have food and shelter in a civilized community that speaks our language. Our team will follow the orders of NASA for samples and documenting this location of Mars. Thanks, back to you Dan". Dan Miller looked put out. NASA was a success. The president is proud.

Mark approached the escort center doors. He scanned the parking lot for coworkers. He wore a suit that was expensive, his output was high in the company of Louis. He had money to buy and his team would pick it up, his business made money and product was in high demand He signed a paper for an escort. He felt sleazy, yet it was a good business maneuver in which he lost his wife 8 months ago. The competition was very strong with him, a relationship with business, the other business was usually civil. They became very extravagant at punch jokes against organizations that were successful. They were very distasteful at disease that ate at the core of the nervous system. He filled out the papers, the sale meeting was in 2 hours. She was to be his date and promote him and his business. She work a pretty evening dress splashed with color. She was very pretty and her build was real well. She ate low fat and had a high output for exercise. His age was 53. Mark Louis was a very handsome business man. She introduced herself, "Hi, I'm Tammy Young." She smiled a smile that held warm hints of sea breeze. "Hi, I'm Mark Louis." They got into his car. "I need to be false for a while. The competition is very fierce. Henceforth, I need a date that gives her positions away as nothing but a loyal date. If the other business are smart at responses, all you have to say is you're with me. I ask that you get hired out to the competition not as an escort service. I assume your service can protect you when you get back" "You have a date Mark Louis" Tammy stated.

The meeting went well. Tammy state the banquet was well and the speaker addressed topics to promote. Tammy was a pro Mark presented well gift booklets were handed out well, boutique executive coffee, hot tea, with honey and wine. The baskets were placed together by the company's president, Mark Louis. The vice president presented a sales report. The sales were good. The salesmen were good. The company was executive 100%. Mark Louis presented well. The food was seasoned well down to desserts and coffee gourmet with a high output of caffeine with rich extras from the estate of Hawaii, Brazil and rich fertile soils around the world. The flavors were extracts that was expensive. Mark knew the price he owned the coffee crop and production of it, he owned the major coffee companies bought by him from the state. He garnished gourmet coffees with rich oils and extracts once the coffee was mature and before harvest. The coffees grew in rich soils around the world. He created a program for quick growth of crops. He manufactured a crop into grocery into wines, honey and hot teas. He owned restaurants and his housing was expensive. Mark sampled the coffee and searched the room his dark eyes watched as hot teas, coffee with rich extracts from al around the world was enjoyed. His coffees were coded by another company and automatically through time only he knew of it. Joe Friedman sampled the coffee, a French vanilla. "I never liked gourmet because it was reduced to decaf. I prefer a sugar free butterscotch." The coffee was loaded with caffeine. Tammy sipped on a margarita tea the exotics made up for the no alcohol drink. She liked it with cream and sugar compared to the 80 90 20000. The tea would be worth 100 dollars a cup. The companies output was 100%. Tammy provided a safety net against fix up relationship and false rumors. She presented well provided well, curtsied well and presented female well. The company was presented well. The executives was presented well from sales people. The executives were caught up with procedures of the company. Papers were handed out on protocol of the company. The company would issue the orders and gain with a high output. The company was very successful.

Bill Myers

"Hi, I am Bill Myers across town Mark Louis hired an escort service to take the place of a date. I guess he thought that he would hide his relationship". Bill was a portly man and wore a black vest. He was a son of an executive and was spoiled rotten. He was groomed for business and money making. His output was high and hair was short and groomed unruly. He carried 30 pounds of extra weight and had high charisma. His computer picked up every business in 100%. He lit up civilizations of New York to Los Angeles. He could place his finger on a red button and the business was bought. If the business failed, he could sell it and break even if it was complete. He had that business agreement because he was fair in business assets. He was a cutthroat with computers and spared no mercy.

"My wife, Linda Bowlin", Bill Myers announced. She was very exquisite in detail. He looked out; he was portly in a black vest. "I got her fresh off a car lot." The woman sneered "Why? His secretary Tina stated you are a pig." He looked at her from dark eyes. The format of the meeting defused from mark Louis. He was business, he knew the computers sells. He would use their product if it were quietly opposition usually thought that it took from their family to use other companies product. He state it is good product only, and use it if he liked it.

"Again," Myers stated, "I got my wife off a car lot. I changed her name none because she was named after a car." He ran his hand through her brown hair. Drug dealers liked iguana and tarantula, exotic animals. "Sexual harassment" said Sue, one of the executive's secretaries. He looked at her, "do you think that I..."he stated with charisma, "am dumb?" He stated like a comedian that emphasized himself well. "No you have a lot of money" He looked at her like she was a little girl. "Are you my accountant?" "No!" Sue stated. She thought that she had him and was a goddess facial, her body was pert. She used expensive emollients only. "My accountant handles my finances." She state with a sneer, all of Myers women were very good looking. He pointed to her, "You wear slinky underwear!" His black vest fit his portly frame. She smiled "Do not!" and spoke to his secretary, "Tina, you better get him good, because he's coming after me now." She smiled. Her exercise routine kept her reflexes quick. Sue stated "Sock him!" She threw punches like a pretty woman. "Sock Him!" She stated again. She really believed that the secretary could charge. Myers looked sideways like Sue was a little girl that fell. Sue took a drink of a coffee is that a beverage that supports Louis and his quality growth of coffee, a stimulant that could be responsible for mental illness because people stay up all night and worry about the day. Sell it, do not support Louis, who may or may not enjoy our product. I would rather sell product to anyone but. Myers was careful as he took the coffee and poured it out. "What do you have on sexual harassment? Nothing! Do you know that it degrades and I am not degrading, am I?" Myers pointed to Linda and stated "Am I?" "No." Linda stated, "You are very nice." "There you have it! Very nice!." Linda was a super model for a car dealership not an escort like Mark Louis had. "Sorry Bill" Sue and Tina apologized.

Montana

The western town of Montana was very full, the people of the 1800's in Timber Lake, ran restaurants, saloons, stores and sheriff's offices. The town was teeming, churches was full and gave God gratitude for their bounty and workmanship. The schools were full and the crops were usually good. The farmers tried to store vegetables and marmalade in glass jars, henceforth if the farmers had a bad crop, the stored food carry them.

The sheriffs stayed in town to protect the town. The marshals were employed by the state. The law was trained high in the early 1800's to protect and settle disputes. Their intelligence was high, their marksmanship was high with weapons.

The ranches were owned by big families. The cattle came from Butte, Montana. A livestock barn herded cattle in from calves. The farmers called them feeders, which meant they fed them from calves and sold them for slaughter or fattening them up. The cattle was henceforth fed on green pastures and upon selling them, herded in on horseback and auctioned off.

Tim Owens

Tim Owens had a ranch and a farm. He had ten sons that worked the ranch and tended to the crops. The farther outside of town, the more difficult to educate the kids and pick up supplies. Tim Owens lived 3 miles out of town. The town ran a stagecoach to pick kids up. The kids were educated well if the parents let them stay in town at boarding houses, work for their rent with chores and ride the state stagecoach home on weekends. The education helped with the ranch work and managing the ranch. The work was hard, yet the ranches helped the town and food abundantly.

The South hunted for deer. They had cows that produced milk and crops. The Southern farmers were great marksmen with pistols, rifles and knives. The stock degraded or something. The cows had worms, the milk was not pasteurized and Southerners got sick. The deer meat did not fatten them up. The cornbread stuck and harvest was hundred miles of shelled beans and corn. The South thought that they suffered from plagues, etc. and it was bad food.

The War Between the States started. The Southerners rode stagecoaches and horses to the west. Sheriff Bob Richardson was domestic to Carson City. His education was well established. He settled disagreements well and was very good with a gun. A Confederate solider had two holstered guns and on Saturday evening he sat in a saloon in Carson City. "Hi!" he stated, Southern drawl presented. He walked up to the bar. The bartender looked him over. "Are you a leprechaun?" "No I am a Southerner from Birmingham, Alabama." "That's a long ride" inquired the Sheriff. "Yes it most certainly is Sheriff" "Why are you here?" the sheriff insisted. "I thought I might ride out here to look the country over." "Are you one of the Confederate army, that military forming down South to dominate the United States?" "Most definitely!" he stated. "The war is between Abraham Lincoln, the cavalry and the South." The Confederate army solider smiled. He was an Irish lad with Southern ways. "Move on!" The sheriff demanded, "you swear allegiance to another president and state." "Yes Sir!" the Confederate solider moved towards the door. His had produced a weapon that put a plug on the forehead of the sheriff. A slit opened red on the sheriffs forehead and he fell over dead. Gun smoke was produced thickly. The Confederate army generals robbed the bank of gold and notes, he left the president dead and two tellers. His horse took him out of town quickly. The Confederate army robbed the United States completely. The sheriffs and marshals were law abiding citizens that went by criteria and laws passed by the state. The Confederate army was crude and tactful against the State. The cavalry made it seldom in time. The gunplay was a war zone. The holstered guns held steel pistols that was reach for, for protection. If they were quick, they live. How they wore the holster that held the gun was according to riding and the style of the gun company. The west was taken by surprise. The only outlaws were listed confederate army soldiers that robbed the 1800's United States. Usually the defense was high. The names that carried from the west and days a long time ago were none little. The criminals were the

Confederate army that robbed the United States a long time ago. Time held on quick draw that was the South presenting weapons against the populace of the Untied States. The names of illegal came and went, the marshal and sheriffs were slain and the country robbed. The name that made it were false and made up, robbed the country repopulated. The South settled and the Confederate army died of old age

NASA

NASA was most impressive on arrival at location of space one location of the 9 planets played the United States on their satellites precisely. It was a review of NASA astronauts. The review of family and a brief report of the United States. NASA knew that the United State reported their expeditions and that their main team was buried in the artic. The team was successful in all events except the enemy or ally undecided yet knew 100% all of NASA exploration. The location was very future and took NASA in 100%. The copy was complete. This location remanufactured NASA's spade and copied Saturn, Mars, 3 locations of space from the United States photo, the farthest reaching planet that could turn to ice because it was the furthest from the sun. Trillions of people from this location lived in a compound that was heated and had cubical housing. A theme park surrounded it. It had layers that grew products the rich Saul went down millions of levels. The crops never ran out and the temperature remained well adapted. The military of Pluto copied the United States and aired a story of NASA with all of NASAs crew and could prosecute for anything illegal they felt. The police force was very good in this planet and the state department was very qualified at protection, medicine and education. Pluto hired men and women in their military to equal NASA, if the situation warranted and the United States tried for a take over. Treatment centers were a state process that medicated you with non addictive medications so that you could be taught strategies of the state to think better legally and process result better. Usually people hate it because it meant that you could not process or handle your life. The family night helped the family to recognize the situation and use constructive ways to contend with it. If a customer call group that was all in treatment would meet and the councilor would ask you to identify with your feelings and talk about your problems. You could identify with your personal likes and output maybe for the first time in your life. Usually a parent makes the choices, school systems or your boss. Treatment did not necessarily depict religion. Usually you choose your own religion. The country ran well, yet one of the 9 planets inhabited by NASA copied the United States. The president held specialized meetings with NASA and the military. "Are these locations really in existence? How much will it cost.? Are they more advanced? Are they hostile toward us and can they take over?" the president placed a team to find out and contradict or be prepared for the things that was mentioned.

Dungeons and Dragons was an organization formed in the 1800's with a southern influence of the Confederated army. Their education was Harvard

Business School. Their organization was one trillion. Satan was their leader, their money was good.

The company of Diamond computers sold security A to Z, the most complete computers were distributed well by a company that was second generation wealth. The money usually didn't make it if the parents died. The state foreclosed and the kids could not regain their estates, except to buy the estates back for the price they were worth. It was like getting money from a banking account that was in someone else's name. Their estates went back to the tax department. The president at Diamond was capable of turning over a profit with his own company. He was second generation and paid programmers to output computers programmed well on an assembly line. He was legal and programmed the most expensive, highly detailed computers ever to be manufactured. His entry into computers netted him cash currency A to Z, the best selling computer ever.

Diamond's company was Dungeons and Dragons, on level 3 with a communications that screened out the law enforcement. Diamond would sell sleazy triple X with the worst of sexual explicit material such as animals being used in a variety of forms. Diamond would open a window for illegal 500 million upon the release of Tony Montana. He paid for 925 houses and actors that narrated similar to radio into the movies and 2 people, Stephen Gridler and Mark Lawlor, his right hand man in the mafia at the time. Randy lived in apartment 8 in Monticello after Cindy was placed in freezer units. 2 million FBI women tried to overtake Cindy Crawford and become her. They were assassinated and placed in dumpsters. President George Bush stated wife beaten what Mr. Bush wanted was the movie money. The estates auctioned of Cindy Crawford dead and any family that Randy grew up with dead. Randy was legal. He helped the country and once the movies went through, you never lost money. Randy had Smith and Wesson sub-machine guns that killed off Eastern State nurses and security. The Mad Maidens with a shot of poison. He dropped them from existence with 100% output and he showed no sign his success was 100%. He was the top gun for the mob.

One thing Randy knew was that stage games George Bush announced meant that he would take over the mafia that Randy was the Don of and after the presidency took it over, George Bush would spend the earnings of over 100 trillion of legal dollars that accumulated from the movies and coffee shops of Randy Cappone. Randy was out at a business when a marine that was big, spoke to some friends of Randy's and showed hostility. The Smith and Wesson was unnoticed when the military would show up and ask for money for the president in a very threatening way. Some felt that their life was in danger and the military would kill them if they did not comply. George Bush waited at Washington for a reply and the spendable cash of Randy Cappone, who he thought was a baby in the organization. The marines were dispensed in dumpsters around the White House. George Bush's money was assessed by the tax department through titles Randy had in the government that was valued. Randy had the best, the most expensive way of getting rid of bodies. Randy complied with the government none because there was no charges. He stated "I do not play any games and will not give you a dollar." He killed him off in 3 minutes; one trillion died and did not come back.

George Bush wanted everything of Randy's dead. Randy gained Cindy came back 2 ½ years later. Randy lived at an apartment in Albany at the Fairgrounds. George Bush came back 2 weeks earlier and retired in Minnesota.

Lexington was a lethal poison from the FBI. The Smith and Wesson saved Randy's life from seconds of a shot going to his mind and killing his system and self. All that was alive of a complete staff was a nurse named Sue. She was Cindy Crawford. The next shift was in soon. He stayed, the medicine was anti-depressants and he was not psychotic.

Rattlesnakes showed up none. The serpents were venomous and gave their poison away none. Their owner went through an end of time planet or location overtake and the serpents were place in a recreation computer to gather food as a human did. Their creator came and went years ago and the tribe had a mind of their own. Their mind was that of a serpent, that of a devil. The devils showed up in time none. The rattlesnake tribe lived forever, recreated ad hatched out young.

John Gotti's mafia was one trillion drug dealers and war soldiers. He was an aggressive criminal that ran crime 100% for the Sicilian mafia. The car in New York was like a tank in design. It was designed for a recreation of a Ouija champ form Hell to demonstrated that Satan's ruling was dominant over the species of human. The driver was some warlock or primed goatee of Satan's lore recreated from Hell. Warlocks lost the name when on a fictional basis females witches were more hand had more mystical power when the Confederate army entombed Irish had power of death with Smith and Wesson. The drive of the septic recreation of ouija emblem had a speaker and stated, "The Beast is coming!" The mike boomed to life. The driver looked worse than any phantom the darkness of Death and reevaluations was with him when his mission was complete. The car went to a mechanic and he disappeared.

A mechanic at Bill's Muffler opened it and it smelled like a funeral that of the recreation. The car was welded like a tank. "Hi, John Gotti." Bull Gotti's right hand man from Milwaukee stated, "Any orders?" John Gotti's hair was gray. He was very distinguished Italian, he looked criminal. "You went to church didn't you? And said you served Jesus!" "Milwaukee's finest does not reveal his spiritual life" he looked like a weasel. "How does it benefit the mafia and do not go against me with it". Bull stated, "It won't." The mafia was not religious and served neither God nor Satan. Within days the FBI infiltrated the organization and incarcerated John Gotti and attempted to shut down his one trillion soldiers.

Santa Fe

John's wife spoke to the women of the mafia and asked that they help her and Bull teach John a lesson. Bull had meetings. He presented himself at book club meetings where hot tea was served by the servants to political women of New York, that worked for the mayor. John Gotti had a Hyatt Regency hotel on 3rd Boulevard that reached 30 levels. He wore expensive suits and drove expensive cars. The don modified crime through drugs. Bull appeared at Santa Fe for John's wife. She spoke well of his business. He had 3 restaurants. Only he knew of that. He kept and made one million apiece. He kept them ten years and sold them when he announced them. The claim was, he poisoned the chowder. Voodoo came in from the station of the Mark of the Beast phantom that ran through time and who worked for John Conti's coffee believed the chowder was poisoned. Their trip to the hospital revealed John Gotti owned them. He sold them in two weeks for a profit. The employees of John Conti, sold the chowder at Conti's coffee shop. Randy worked there and through that, the chowder was differential because Voodoo or Black magic bleed from it. Bull winked and asked that the women go his way to teach John Gotti a lesson. Bull wore dark glasses that framed black when his contacts were being cleaned. People recognized him move.

John stated that "I had no power in religion, so I wanted to show him that I did by shutting his drug operations down." He smiled, his Milwaukee charm permeated that he was civilized and only kidding.

"Santa Fe" Bull stated the right hand man of John Gotti was personable. "John does not need to be selling drugs or killing people. I want that incarcerated out." "Is that a wig?" Lyons inquired, feeling her dark half. Santa Fe frowned, "I got my hair styled and cut and want to preserve it." Lyons looked at her, "Your hair is blond. What do you do? Wear a wig, then go out devoid of Mr. Gotti, the Don's ruling?" He shook his finger accusingly in a kind way. "Do not cause any trouble". She looked at house security, "Get him out!" The security wor a white uniform and escorted him out. She sneered, showing pretty outstanding Italian. The wig was supposed to be scolding and stern. She searched the room with eyes. "There's no street wise thug I cannot control" "Hey," Bull stated "Cheezer" Lyons stated at the door. "Tell John Conti that his coffee was good if that water did not destroy it." "Who Randy?" Mark stated with a lot of persona. He liked the coffee and ended up out in the snow and in the hospital and back to Albany, where he reached star statues. He's Al Cappone's son. Lyons left. "Be on my side" Bull suggested.

John Gotti

John Gotti's mafia was seemingly taken over by the FBI. Bull was intent on processing drugs out of time. John Gotti's men were put off on meetings with the Don. His replacement was a smashing resemblance of John Gotti. John Gotti made in and out of jail and underground into the pipes and septic of New York. He lived like an Italian for days and a rodent after weeks past. He broke into houses, shaved and showered and stole food. He listened to conversations. He heard the police move in on his organization. He had to get back somehow and resume his position.

Bull met at book club meetings. He swilled expensive wine high in octane with 32% alcohol. "Hi, Im' Mrs. Myers. My husband is an executive in oil. We have a son, ten. Our interest in New York is high that New York processes barrels of oil well. We like the etiquette of social life and like the way Mrs. Gotti processed John and organized crime syndicates out. We don not need a villain playing off our earnings." Bull swilled his wine tonic. "Absolutely, Mrs. Myers. We want John processed through the judicial system to see what he contains if after his court date the police wan to keep an eye on him, so be it." He tasted the wine. "I thought that you were into God. Why would you drink wine?" Mrs. Gotti caught Bull enjoying a sinful taste of alcohol. "Sorry Mrs. Gotti." Bull handed his wine glass to the next waiter with a tray. "It won't happen again." "Make sure of it!" Mrs. Gotti replied. Bull looked out. "NO, NO, NO!" he replied, "and No, it won't happen again"

Steve Loren

Gotti's FBI replacement looked over blueprints of Gotti's estates that were kept in case he wanted to add on. Gotti's replacement was Steve Loren. He was very educated in criminal law. Gotti's estates were paid for by the restaurants and hotels. His men were very streetwise. He knew that Gotti left the jail and came and went whenever he wanted to. He thought that he was and Steve knew that he was out of business on racketeering and he and his FBI and the New York Police had placed a Don out of business. John Gotti was high profile. A state police officer moved swiftly to John Gotti's jail cell. "John Gotti, come on out!" The cell was opened. "John Gotti, we are going to re-arrest you, you escaped our judicial system and broke into houses. We are going to move you" John was shook down and was issued a court date for the added charges. John Gotti's men were arrested, one hundred at a time and charged with dealing drugs and associating with John Gotti, a racketeer.

The judge looked at Gotti form glasses that fell down his nose. "You! John Gotti, an organized crime leader, are looking at a lot of jail time for racketeering and breaking and entering. How do you plead?" "Not guilty" The courtroom erupted in laughter. "Guilty!" John said "What?" The judge looked down at Gotti and said, "There's only one way out of this for you" "Your honor????" John inquired. "Sign up for Stage games 3 government capability for centralized crime" "I don't have that power of centralized crime" "If you sign for your organization, we will process you through and send you home to play the government". John asked, "Will the charges be dropped?" "If you sign, the charges will be dropped said the Judge. John signed. John's organization was processed 100% and sent home. His finances were gone over with the tax department. The drug money went to the state. John was processed 100% into the state government. John's wife gave him stipulations. Bull smiled and said "Are you straight, John?" John smiled, "Yes Bull" "Okay, I'll go. Put her here!" he said offering his hand. John Gotti shook it, "You are a friend Bull." Bull slid out the door. 'It's good to have you back. I am happy Santa Fe had blond hair." "You, my dear, are not Southern." John placed his index finger on her nose. Mrs. Gotti reached for the phone and punched in the numbers. "Police department." "What are you doing?" John asked. "Hi, this is Santa Fe Gotti. John was incarcerated and he thinks that he's my boss. Could you check him out?" Bull appeared with a gun. "John Gotti, your crime boss days are over!" "Bull, those corduroy pants are out of date, you look like a matador." "You are going to jail, my friend. Santa Fe, do you want anything form him? You can take it." "Absolutely, a 100 dollar United States processed bill." The police arrived. "Good!" Bull stated "He called me a matador and I want confiscation." "Where did you get that gun!" the police asked Bull. Bull was placed under arrest. "You can't take money from him Mrs. Gotti. He has to be fined by the state. Here," he handed it back. "If your wife wants you reprocessed, you as a crime leader are going to be processed." Bull was sent to jail for 2 weeks because he had a gun. John Gotti was processed in 3 hours.

The military camped out around John Gotti's house. Stage 3 meant the government got to test John Gotti to see if he could back his organization. You had to sign and you got to give things up to the government. The state department urged that the family not go around them. They called it a male menstrual. John Gotti stated, "I don't have one!" The military checked him out. The state police and everyone he harmed would come back on him with state protection. Santa Fe would leave soon. If the state could, they would execute everything of John Gotti's including his family. The state watched to make certain no one came in the lives. Stage 3 was a death wish. Nobody ever won and the saying stated no one ever escaped from Alcatraz. John Gotti was processed by the state police. He spoke to the tax department. "My name is Lena. I would like to look at your assets 20 years later."

Mrs. Gotti was blond and built well. "I would love to claim a coffee shop for my son. John Gotti, the factory employee spoke to the tax department. "Okay, your coffee shop is claimed. Don't come back or we state crude about your coffee. It's legal. John was 3 years old His dad adopted a company of John Conti gourmet coffee. He stole a package and process from a large company that was processed through time. The year was trillion exon. John went back 3 weeks later. Why? Because the tax department was cute. The announcement on the president communication was "John Gotti and the John Conti coffee company went out on tax evasion."

If you would have had a communication and stated Randy Cappone, he stayed at his parents' house during the Confederate overtake.

"Did you issue a team of Sicilian mafia on the company and tax evasion?" Cindy Crawford would have come on communication, a phone with video and looked like Lacinda, a waitress that worked with Randy before he was sent to Eastern State.

The company was into computer demoniacs not witchcraft because it modified death. Cindy would have then turned into herself. She was very pretty. "Did you send a team back to the future of Exxon?" "Absolutely! The mafia was sent back one hour to show John Gotti, John Conti coffee company was distributed by John Conti. He bought coffee from whatever company at what ever price he wanted. I picked up Starbuck and Millstone and John Conti, he was paid 100%. The decafs are decaf and the regulars are regular in caffeine. The team was one hour and lasted one hour. It was called "get John Gotti out of our hair for awhile" John Gotti said that he wanted to go out on tax evasion. The team went on trillion years. The idea was to get rid of John Gotti for a day. He was gone an hour" "You lost on tax evasion because you came back and I ask you not to. The company of John Conti, you r son was stolen, the original company was Starbuck". The United States 2000 Starbuck coffee was 100 caffeine distributed to Americans by Randy Cappone. He bought the company form the state department. The products sold.

John Gotti went home. He lost his son's company. The coffee company of John Gotti's was Evasave and stayed open. It was a death company. The Gotti's were paid for by the state. The Gotti's felt they were cursed. The company killed their customers because they lost on tax evasion. The gotti's had poison, knives and guns. The state could not shut them down. The family was paid for by the state and went through trillions of years. The dominant male at 70 went out and received Satan and died with the Mark of the Beast. The coffee company showed up in time none, not even to Satan. His service was almost as much automatic. The company went on trillions into the future. The family was cursed by John Gotti's tax evasion. "How are you ?" John Gotti asked Randy Cappone. My tax evasion journey is through. John wore an expensive suit. He said Hi to Cindy. Cindy was a doll to the mafia from the first time she supermodeled or bacme a super model and married and divorced Richard Gere. They were proud that she and Randy were married and had a son, Colt. John Gotti shook Randy's hand. "Exxon too me out on taxes" John smiled. "You know the reason I put up with you and accept you as the boss" "Why?' Randy asked. "Because you're Al Cappone's son and distribute the mafia well" Gotti stated. "Keep him straight Cindy!" John left

George Bush presented himself on his communication from Washington to Monticello. "Who wants to play Stage 3 Games?" Randy took the president's communication and processed it through programmers and it opened up with screens to Hawaii and Cappone estates where Randy and Cindy Crawford and Colt live in a trillion dollar mansion. "I do not play stage games!" Cindy stated, "Please tell the president, you don't play." After Randy said that, he went and froze the family 100% and played the government out of everything. Randy stated "Because the president met and modified around speaking unkindly of me. I was not running for anything."

The overtakes were modified to look like President George Bush, the first after the administration went to zero was Fidel Castro. He looked like president George Bush. There were administrations one after another. Lisa, the head programmer, held Randy's picture by a computer conjunction of a program designed by Randy. He got into all ends of time and changed appearance whenever he needed.

The apartment at Hillcrest Monticello sat behind a convenience store the mafia had keys to open them up. The computer printout read the biggest criminal of all time was created a Black Tarantula that was created by a state department that wanted to create a venomous spider to weed time out of crime. The crew worked the insect through. He was aggressive and ate the enemy 100%. The team that create him went out to eat. He roamed around crawling. The computer instructed by the company was to make certain there was no crime in this location. The location came and went, the highest number on quarto with 100 zeros time ago civilizations ago. Billion in the past. Time and civilization came and went, the computer registered that this criminal never lost. He was dried up and gone trillions of years ago before Satan, before God, he controlled 100% of his locations. Randy recreated him and incorporated him as his right hand man. Upon being introduced to his time, he found out that the team that created him was illegal. He killed the team. They did not get their classifications legalized and were killed by a dominant male Black Widow. The government, state official called him in and he killed the state department 100%. The state department and locations had trillion of people. It was Gotham. The criminal was Joker. He was recreated by Randy as his right hand man. He extended the mafia that Randy was the head Don of and Al Cappone stated during the 1920" by 100 years at least.

Cindy was in Hawaii. Randy was at his parents in Albany. The movie sales were high. It was a good package for Randy to become a writer, director and actor in Scarface, Tony Montana. The movie sales were high, Randy and Cindy were very prestigious in the movie business. Cris Penny was Branndons' mom. Her dad was a man that hit a big well in Albany and made millions. She was Branndon, Randy's oldest son's mother. The 5 played it as a team. Branndon and Colt were Al Cappone's grandsons. The kids were 5 years different in age.

Randy and Cindy Crawford did well for 2 people that received lethal poison by the state department, while Randy was in Lexington. There were no charges. The apartment 8 in Monticello was a plug for Al Cappone's only son, Randy, that was trained by Mr. Cappone's mafia his whole life. The mafia could over take any instillation and carry through Al's orders in seconds.

Cindy's estates had food replenishments and protection units 100%. George Bush met with every powerful congress and politician in Washington. He cam on his sublime communication that activated a military in war zones and ask people if they wanted to play stage 3 games. When Randy was asked, he stated. "I do not play, because we are a real organization that kills". That meant the mafia broke any organization down that met to overcome them and they did not come back. George was communicating through a sublime communications that petocolded your memories being burnt after transations that breed devils and demons form Dusk Till Dawn. It was computer generated protocol, it came on mental disease stress and tension. The state department took over and became the people in your lives through the military, the FBI. The president could drop and become the United States and process money. "Mr. Bush," Randy stated. "You will play stage games" During President

Obama's presidency, Randy had one trillion mafia soldiers, George Bush did not exist. "Good morning, Mr. Bush" President Obama held the phone close to his ear. "Good morning. I lost some weight" George Bush replied. "Boy," Obama started "The mob lost you in time. You're supposed to show arrest and breakdowns in an organization. Randy killed your military when you sent them to Monticello. The team never made it back. Over 500 marines went out of Monticello, Kentucky in a body bag. You thought that Randy Cappone was weak and you could take him. He took you and turned your money in. You are second generation political." George Bush had curly hair. He looked like an eagle, an aggressive politician like his father. "I thought that Randy was edited in Don and that the mafia backed him through Al Cappone. I did not know that he had guns." Mr. Bush stated. "He processed you" Obama stated.

The Gotti organization was A to Z crime of New York. The crime organization followed John Gotti's orders precisely. His output was good. He answered to Al Cappone 100%. Al Cappone, the 1920's mafia was the same his brother John Gotti, died 3 times form the 20's to today. He always went by the name John Gotti because it was his name. Lexington, Kentucky was a war area, the gates of Eastern State were locked. The Rattlesnakes community would come. The organization of Rattlesnake was the most deadly of any organizations, some called them of Satan's organization tribes. The Rattlesnakes were deadly most organizations were state tribes played Voodoo that melted the mind and eventually wore off. The mafia was point blank killers. The Cappones won because they were aware of danger ad poised the Rattlesnake tribe or organization of devils, became your organization of Satan and bit e you with fury and took your body out dead.

Cindy stayed at an apartment in Lexington. Their communications was a phone company line that was progressed through time it was 100% communications. Cindy came into the psychiatric hospital in complete disguise and only helped. Lexington was a location that was supposed to be a horror zone, a tragic location of Satanism and w victims, Cindy and Randy. However, Randy did not want to die. Everyday was a horror beyond belief. Randy called for the mafia. John Gotti stated that he could have it, be processed crime against people that tried to kill him 100%. John Gotti, a Sicilian was considered light by some. However he was tough. His organization could take the state of New York quick. Stage 3 was warfare with foreigners. JFK was killed by Cuba. Abraham Lincoln an example, signed for Stage 3 and meant the war was pretended yet the Confederate army retaliated upon being told that the was an easy victory. President Bill Clinton signed for Stage 3 with the Confederate army. Randy Cappone was in apt. 8. He moved from his parent's house into it and overnight asleep. Mark Lawlor stated that it was an easy war with the Confederate army. Saturn came in to test Randy's right hand man Mark Lawlor. The war with future civilizations that supported the deceased Confederated army went on for 2 ½ years. Randy ordered a new mafia while Al Cappone, Mark Lawlor, Steve Grider and a million Dons were frozen. Cindy Crawford, Randy's wife returned 2 ½ years later. Randy's new right hand man was the Joker, an Emperor Black Tarantula that became the enemy by eliminating the enemy and his team to present day, Joker was the new best, Mark was second. Werewolves were uncannily evil as a beast that changed and broke in and killed superstition and laire the maddening of love that was usually slotted Halloween and output of evil anything that proceeded in God, green Earth and according to the state God existed or churches of variety would exist none. Controlled churches because had to keep the laws of the United States. All state offices had to go by laws of the United States and performed protection from crime with the police force. The state department controlled all state offices and were funded by the United States. To be safe as a United States citizen, you had to have police protection, that also meant security that was had from a security service educated by the state and competent of laws by the state. Lexington held criminal 100% from the time Randy wound up in Eastern State Hospital. The crime was Lexington went to Satanism and to kill Randy and Cindy. Both played Lexington well for their own lives. Smith and Wesson was dropped, the noise was minimized and the sub-machine guns dropped out of state and could be found none. Rattlesnakes were devils unaccounted for in time. The tribe took over Eastern State Hospital 100%. The Vipers were underestimated in time 100% There was a Rainbow Tarantula, cobras and a variety of venom beyond belief. It was a death zone beyond belief. The stars were distant forever was beyond processes of time. The Environment tasted of Venom and death was not a pretense. The teams were to melt back in time with no proof after Randy was killed, Christmas came while the incarceration happened. Randy received Christmas socks from a state mission. The ideas promoted between him and Cindy was excellent. They were like two people dying in a coal mine with a bag that if breathed in, saved their lives. They liked each other a lot.

"Stage is on if you play." George Bush announced. Randy spoke directly to George Bush. "I don't ply stage, our organization is real. We don't play government games". Cindy from the estates in Hawaii stated "I don't play" George Bush stated "Okay" Randy went into his apartment. He had an aquarium that was small and had two fish, both were neon. The filter filtered out impurities. It was the first time a small inexpensive aquarium stayed clean and worked. Randy was raise don a farm that produced soy and corn, pigs, cows and a garden full of tomatoes and corn. The goldfish form Kmart, the main store in Marion, Indiana, died within days from the water. He bought a parakeet, a blue Budgie that lived 5 years. This 10 dollar aquarium bought in the town he lived in, filtered out impurities and maintained the neon fish. George Bush is modifying around and states that he wants money. "Freeze me in Cappone freezer units and bring me back when you modify him out." The bed was delivered by a furniture company in Albany. Randy froze his wife, Cindy Crawford 2 days. She was in Hawaii and he was in Monticello, KY.

"Have relationships, remarry, set the estates to go through time. Kill the president and bring me back. I love you". It was the last time he saw her for 2 ½ years. He loved her very much.

George Bush spoke unkindly of Randy in feminine ways. He tried for a stage game counsel. He wanted Randy dead, his family dead, Cindy dead, Cris Perry dead and his sons, Brandon and Colt. Randy was in the back of a huge crowd. The stage game counsel was supposed to execute the president's orders. There were no charges. The president announced Randy Cappone is under Stage 3, meaning complete ruin for a male. The mafia started by Al Capppone was frozen in time. What the president wanted was to modify around, send the military in with weapons and kill Randy.

The Rattlesnake tribe killed an organization that reported in to their leader none. The tribe killed. Satan would pick them up at the end of time. They killed when someone was too far out and ate the victims. The Snake tribe killed when the state said they could. Their form was the enemy's organization. Venom blinded them. The announcement was Randy had a base that modified to Sabine Tiger called White Wing that emulated from a classic pirate movie. By computer junction, he did an imprint and copied the organizational tribe of Satan. George Bush was President. Randy's last occupation was waitering at a family restaurant. He was outgoing in physical work. He ate low fat 5 days a week, Monday through Wednesday, regular on Thursday and Sunday and low fat on Friday and Saturday. The total number of low fat days was 500. He was his own weight. He stayed at his parent's house. There was no area he didn't get into during the Confederacy overtake, he was AAA. Mark Lawlor was good. Steve Grider was good and Al's record was high. The hostage total was high. Randy developed systems and brought them in safely. He fed America when they could not feed themselves. During the floods down South, he sent food. His record was AAA. The organization that backed him was the Sicilian mafia. He was head Don over the organization. Their output was high. Lexington led with organizations such as Dungeons and Dragons. The state department led with Illegal to absorb Randy and Cindy. Upon leaving Albany, Randy asked the state police and sheriffs department to take him to Lexington. There were no charges. The FBI ordered an illegal state of execution for him. He dropped the poison staff with sub-machine guns. The bodies were out. Cindy Crawford became a nurse, he was in Eastern State. In 3 weeks, he went to Louisville. After he was released and he was placed back in. He developed systems to kill and bring the enemy back automatically. After Eastern State Hospital, Randy was sent to the Hope Center for the Homeless.

George Bush had a crowd, the stadium was full. "Hi! It's George Bush. Randy Cappone was incarcerated with a speeding ticket going 83 miles an hour. We incarcerated him through a deputy sheriff at the Wayne County line. He was arrested for Racketeering and incarcerated after being turned over to the Somerset police department. He was place under arrest for racketeering. One trillion of his mafia went to jail and await trial. His finances was and is trillions. He programmed and maneuvered past the Confederate army, the biggest army from Hell. He and Cindy Crawford, killed with weaponry. The state department of Lexington, no one came forward as a witness against the crime teams. I want to bring his victims back to confront him with a fighting chance." He swung his fist in the air like a boxer. "Al Cappone backed his son with a gun. He's in a freezer unit. Randy has no backing with his mafia incarcerated. He did not sign for Stage 3, that means the government tests you on your ability to overcome it. You have to sign at a state police office and the military breaks you down and your local police department. You play the government and it comes off the day you die. The military kills you with poison" George held the microphone tight. The crowd was hushed. "Cindy Crawford was frozen and the FBI tried to infiltrate. 2 million female FBI agents were killed and placed in dumpsters." It lit up on the screen. Randy dropped them using his expertise with weapons. A man that looked like a viper with blue eyes ad medium build was shown. "That's Randy Cappone, killing them over time and he made it back to Hillcrest Apartment 8. This ghastly crime went without charges" The screen went blank. Randy stood with cuffs on. "I want him to pay " George stated. He looked like the President of the United States in a blue suit. "Take the cuffs off" Randy was place in a chute and George sneered. :"You are under scrutiny of the United States government." The Running man, Randy was placed in a chute that would go into the tunnels of New York, where he could fight the Races. George looked at him with a sneer. "We'll see!" Randy stated, "I'll win!!!" "In Hell" George stated. The ride was activated down a tunnel. The morning came to life, Randy's endurance was 100%. The military watched the games. The Cuban administration on a level 3 because the Bush administration took over. Bush stated, "I don't care. I want the mafia out of commission. I gave them permission". The Cuban administration was good at warfare. The hostile nations from the Middle East put their masks on. It was like a ribbed metal catchers mask. They hid in jungles and produce high in warfare. They wanted the mafia out of commission. No war zone or state police ever really knew how to behave with the mafia. The Middle East fought wars that did not show up in time.

What George Bush wanted was everything of Randy's dead. The black magic was a fog that was beyond belief. Cindy showed up with Richard Gere stating they were back together. The fog was shadows of the nigh he saw her take off with Wagner. He called him Bruce. It was a cut, five guys laughed and spoke the.44 killed all of them, the bodies erased. He spoke to Shania Twain about re-entering his house apartment 8. She helped him. The dream dilemma and current reality faded. He woke up with Cindy on his mind. Shania left messages on Randy's movie line. "Good morning. Please return my message". He smiled, he liked her, she was built AAA. He returned her call. The kids were at leas t 500 when Cindy came out of the freezer units with Cris Perry, Brandon and Colt. "Welcome Back" Randy smiled. He communicated with them from the fairgrounds. "Did you sign in government for Stage 3?" It meant the government tested you and you went against the government. Cindy smiled "I don't know what it means". He smiled welcome back.

The government games were excruciating if incarcerated, you had to sign in the government and the president would take you to his personalized of communication in the mornings, he would wave his arms and say let's go. The person would play and when done he would wave sideways and it would go off by computer and say on if you think you're my boss.

When Randy went to Monticello, President George Bush stated wife beating. Randy knew that he froze her for a day. George Bush started procedures to prosecute from the White House on wife beating. Randy's programmer loaded in Randy becoming the enemy. She typed in a program. "You can become the enemy." "Thanks Lisa" "What's the matter Cappone ? You usually love situations like this." He smiled. Apartment 8 faced an old garage in the back. Sometimes they fired up a sports car. He thought that it was too loud for city ordnance. He got the cable hooked up. He missed Cindy. From Hawaii, she was supportive during the Confederate overtake. Cindy said to re-marry and have more kids. That was because you were an only son and you could incorporate more Sicilian mafia. "That's right. I have a hole in my stomach. I miss her" Randy stated. "I've loaded in the Best of Marriage and Cappone stock". She could be Cindy's cousin and programs of the Running Man bought and government approved and quantum leap then billion dollar programs. Your strategy and output will be outstanding. Al Cappone and the mafia are frozen except no doubles incorporated by the FBI. You're coded in the reload is automatic and the enemy is replaced automatically. You showed no sign and the law cannot incorporate any system you are Sicilian law and the head Don. The Bush administration was edited in for the most of the Gulf war. It was almost impossible to find planes that could cross millions of miles into the ocean without refueling. Randy was capable because his planes were constructed into the future. He could get ingot war zones and become characters that he called it. Characters was to become someone are without being recognized and absorbing the enemies and infiltrating their organization and the mafia becoming the enemy. He developed future systems A to Z characterizations were a freezer location. The people or person got into freezer units or the organization and came out in almost mechanical bodies. Randy could go into any location in seconds and demand results. Al Cappone found the situation out and when he reached consciousness he killed the leaders. He was 100% with the State. Yet he was tagged the biggest criminal of all time and somehow gained by that. He lived through time since the 1920's, the mafia was tough and knew who was the enemy was and won 100% of the time they were a tough military that sold drugs and illegals. Lexington, KY was full of devils at Eastern State someone named Bruce came in. He wore a white collar and a suit. Randy asked if he was a minister. He went Randy's way on most everything, except he was a minister of death. He was Bruce Tombs from the tombs of Hell. Eastern State was a lockdown ward that went though chambers the institute had been in admission for a long time. The staff had been given the orders for a state of execution by the FBI. They would honor it with lethal poison. The ward was locked down, the location contained death and execution. Randy thoughts were good with the exceptions he had a program, a package governed by the presidency that controlled a break down of old government with a protocol. Computers that went through your mind, the computer overtook with Ouija, Black magic and programs that dissolved the functions of your brain. You could not process it because it over rode your mind. If you adopted habit of workmanship, you gained the mechanism, would override your psychic, it was a computer or an output that produced an overtake of the psychic. It was a breakdown in processing 100% of a political establishment that came and went. It had no practical functions except to break down your psychic. The real question was where the computer came from and how to process it. Upon the presidency ending, the other president took over and the protocol computer was activated by the new president. It had no mind except to break down old political. It was modified outdated and useless to the United States code of ethics. It left no traces. Randy left the house. His thumb was up and it was raining. He did not know where the government computer came from. He caught a ride into Albany, KY. It's raining. It's the end of time. He processed poorly. The FBI was in Albany to process from Louisville, a convention and to see Al Cappone's son who went by a different name and had no information of being a relative of the Sicilian mafia, one of the biggest crime organizations ever. Randy went in to a family business. The people were shadowed, the person that he caught a ride with was affiliated with law enforcement. The waitress asked if he wanted something to drink and he said no and left. Hours later he caught a ride with a waitress he worked with. He was not educated to know where the government protocol computer came from.

The United States was loaded into an underground world after President Bill Clinton signed for Stage 3 war fare with the Confederate army. General Grant signed. The FBI was the one that was to process poison for the U. S. A. One of the FBI officials pointed to Al Cappone, "Joseph hold on that's Al Cappone!" It was months after Lexington President Bill Clinton was under ground. He lost control of the process. "Leave them!" Cindy stated, "they come after you at the end of your administration and try to process you out when the president says you are under scrutiny, Randy knew that end of regency meant a foreign power would over take". Randy knew of variations of the Confederate army overtake, he learned about it in Lexington and reported it to John Conti. The process of end of regency meant the state tried to over take foreigners. They had to have charges and you had to go before a judge with any other accusations.

The New Presidency

Randy Cappone was in apartment 8. Cuba was defeated and he knew the difference in Level One and Two. He was exquisite at war. President George Bush woke up in his oval office and stretched. The United States military was called to war against Randy. The Army, Marines, Navy and all corps were armed. The country thought that Randy was light and Al Cappone's Sicilian mafia was the toughest. Randy was tough with Mark Lawlor and Grider. Overnight he rebuilt one trillion Italians for the mafia. Those that went to the penitentiary were mechanical. His right hand man, Mark Lawlor and ex-military Stephen Grider were frozen. The government was after the Sicilian mafia. He was head Don and trained them.

Randy was an aspect of the presidency and George Bush's protocol war zone meetings. He killed the president time and again and he came back from freezer units. President George Bush bequeathed Saturn, most populous of the planets. There was 100 trillion civilized people that froze for millions even trillions for one day. The forces were end of time similar to the Confederate army. His messages stated "This Shania Twain, your new men are competent". The next day they work up in states. He copied states 1000 times and it was progressed to come back. Shania kissed him, she spoke seldom. Her country music career taught her to remain quiet.

"How did Randy get away?" George Bush asked the military general, Tim Gates. "Sir, Randy Cappone built strategies in government to evade. We will apprehend him." "Very good." George Bush stated.

John Gotti loved cases that were tough against the Sicilian mafia of New York. He was very good at government strategy and gained most of the time the state thought that he was goofy and he was a killer. The Bush administration was uneventful during his presidency. He had little political power. Randy Cappone, Mark Lawlor, Steve Grider and Al Cappone fought the war from Albany, Kentucky. George got involved none. He would try to conduct business and his own team that registered one trillion would leave the location. Randy Cappone fought the war over the Confederate army and gained. George Bush regained his military after a crack job was done. The military regained power upon Randy's move to Monticello. He redistributed the government back to the president. The mafia was distributed into freezer units for future assignment. States was a future that returned and remained inactivated. The process was a get away for Randy against any enemy. He produced games beyond time. The Administration of George Bush came and went and President Obama wanted to play the mafia. They were legal and won against end of time forces and was adored by America for valor and output in the movies. The presidencies of Obama and Bush came and went like a quiet whisper on a heated summer night. The company was rehired and when they came out of freezer units the Don's were retired. Randy took over the strategies of the mafia and legally obtained the military and state office and kept them

Stan Brewster

Stan Brewster was a registered agent of the FBI. He was from Milwaukee. His favorite thing in life was history because we won in history. He, as a FBI agent loved stage because you bothered someone until they did something if they did not give in the first time they were free. Stan met in Louisville, KY with two million FBI agents and when the convention was over, the organization went to Albany, Ky to see Randy Cappone.

Lisa Anderson was a very well built waitress. Later to be edited as Bruce Willis in "Die Hard" started to the waitress that brought eggs to him. "You smell of patties and feminine hygiene." The place looked at him and stated "why don't you have a patty sandwich, one for you and one for me." The two became friends forever.

Brewster went back twice a day. He showed her his badge one day. "Keep it. I know that you take people underground and only process the ones that give in to protocol 3. Randy Jones who became Randy Cappone had nothing in your area. They tried shock treatment and he would not accept them." "Keep your badge. He'll go after the government someday and win." Brewster smiled

"The government's wrong to go in any one mind. Protocol or no protocol." She was for Randy. He was for the government as a state employee. Brewster said, "Please marry me." Three times later he proposed with flowers and candy. She said yes and he gave her a ring. The last thing he said was if Randy Jones proposed would you have accepted? She married him because he stated FBI business or I will process you underground. He went to work in Washington everyday, 8 hours a day he was the lead captain of the FBI. The reason he took Lisa underground and poisoned her was he preferred his sex kinky and thought that she would win him. Three weeks later Stan and Lisa were married 3 years when he fed her poisoning. Brewster was in Albany, Ky to meet Al Cappone's son. Lexington police department opened to Stan Brewster. "What charges do you have", Steve Miller, the police captain and State police captain asked. Stan stated, "I want to process him through the state and process crime out." Steve Miller gave Stan Brewster complete leeway of the police in Lexington. The city was sealed off. Stan's first orders were, "I would like to incorporate Bruce Wagner." The uniformed police watched. Stan smiled. If asked Stan thought of his wife that only knew of Stan as a used car salesman. He would look dangerous and if honest, confess that to him, she was a disposable sex toy. That was a complete ruin upon her friends asking about sex and being told that he liked being tied up and completely dominated by a female. Joe Hall, an affiliate of his and an FBI man gave him a high five. The females were poisoned and the very brilliant well built female was not talking. The thing about it was death was permanent. Stan thought of his wife as a win in the FBI organization and very disposable.

"Bruce Wagner, I would like to promote Bruce to our crack law team. Just when you think you are at peace, Bruce runs a line through to promote his Satanist ways. He's the devil himself." Captain Miller called Bruce, Bruce answered the phone. He had brown hair and brown eyes and wore expensive suits. He sneered upon smiling and looked like a rattlesnake. Bruce was picked up by the FBI. He had A to Z venomous snakes, was into organizations of spiders and the worst degenerate killers from the penitentiary. He was Satan to the FBI.